GREEN MACHINE

By RON BRUNK

Green Machine

Library of Congress Control Number: 2013920314

ISBN 978-0-989737-22-7 (eBook)
ISBN 978-0-9897372-9-6 (pbk)

Cover artwork by Brenna Hicks.

Alexia Publishing
PO Box 120942
Nashville, TN 37212
www.alexiapublishing.com
www.ronbrunk.com
ronbrunk@yahoo.com

In Loving Memory of Ted W. Mills.

He died much too young.

Table of Contents:

With wings now dripping blood,
Bird perched upon my soul;
Together he and I
Went deeper in the hole.

– "Vulture"
Michael Crisp (1976)

Emily

The first time I laid eyes on Emily she was throwing darts in a crowded bar & grille in downtown Memphis. I tried not to stare but it was a lost cause. Her eyes were a jagged shade of jade, and her hair was thick and dark as the woods on Pemberton Mountain when the sun goes down. She wore faded bell-bottom jeans and a Greenwich Village tee shirt, and unknowingly sported a dab of barbeque sauce on her chin. When I pointed that out to her, she giggled and I was smitten. We shared a plate of pulled pork, downed a pitcher of beer, then danced and laughed till last call.

Later, we walked beside the silent Mississippi where Emily shined her glorious greens into my eyes and kissed me more tenderly, more passionately than a woman has ever kissed a man. In that single unexpected moment, there was nothing else. There was no half-moon glinting off a quarter parking meter, no juke joints murmuring two streets over, no Canis Major leaping through the night, no muddy river to our right, and, for that moment, no wayward matriarchal ghost to my distant left. We stood there holding hands, midnight blinking worlds away.

Emily and I followed a two-lane road that curled through the mountains like a long, black snake, and I had the feeling that we were slithering up its back toward the fangs of fate in the darkness. The last week, hell, the last five years had blown by like a furious blur. My life was insane. Maybe I was tired of living in the shadow of a star.

That evening, somewhere along Route 30 near the straight-back borderline between Pennsylvania and the West Virginia panhandle, we lay on the hood of my Ford Bronco, eating bologna sandwiches, munching on corn chips – Emily loved her Fritos - and drinking Iron City Beer. A warm wind pushed strands of Emily's dark hair to and fro as the nighttime stars took command of the sky.

"Em, I want to ask you something," I said carefully. "You don't have to talk about it if you don't want to."

She popped a chip in her mouth and smiled. "Ask me anything, mister man."

"How did you get that scar on your cheek?"

My question clearly took her by surprise, but it was something I'd wondered about since that first night. In my estimation, the scar gave her *something*, something dark and powerful that I could not quite put my finger on, something that, in some mysterious way, enhanced her already abundant charms and simple beauty.

There was an airplane in Orion's belt and we watched in silence as it crawled across the great hunter's chest and leaped off his shoulder.

"My father cut me with a broken bottle," Emily said finally, eyes still fixed on the stars. She put a hand up to her face absently and traced the faint, crescent moon-shaped line.

"What? My God, do you mean…intentionally? Why? What happened?"

"I was just a little girl. He was drunk," she said flatly with little emotion. "I don't want to talk about this."

"Okay, that's cool…I understand. I was just curious," I said, nervously backing off.

"So, what's the deal with you?" Emily asked, suddenly turning the tables. "You haven't told me anything about your parents either."

"Not much to tell," I answered. "My mother was a vicious vulture and I hope she's burning in hell right now."

"Damn," Emily said, wide-eyed. "First, you say there's not much to tell; then you unload *that*. Are you kidding me?"

I ignored her comment and pressed on with my family summary. "My father was an asshole, and he and I didn't get along at all. But he's mellowed a bit over the years, and I think we've reached some sort of understanding. Or at least, we tolerate each other."

Emily was still shaking her head at me. "On the bright side," I said. "My grandfather was a great man and I loved him very much. I miss him."

"Back up, back up," Emily said. "You have to tell me more about your mother."

I took a deep breath and said, "My mother was an evil, conniving bitch who resented me from the day I was born. No, let me correct that – she resented me even *before* I was born. She never forgave me for being born five days past my due date, as if that was *my* fault. It wasn't physical abuse like what your father did to you;

13

my mother waged a psychological war, mocking and belittling me, her only son. She sowed seeds of fear and guilt that still bear fruit to this very day."

I finished off my beer and popped the top on another.

"Then she got cancer and used her disease to play the most horrific trick of all on me. I had to watch her waste away and suffer for a year, until she finally pulled me into a devious suicide scheme, making me an unwitting accomplice in her death."

Emily's jaw dropped. "*A suicide scheme*? What do you mean?"

"Ah, forget it. I don't want to talk about my mother anymore," I said. "She's dead and gone. Let's just let it rest there for now."

Emily bit her lip and said, "Okay, then tell me more about your father. Where is he now?"

"Albuquerque."

"Do you ever visit him?"

"Not very often. In my father's house are many demons, some of which I doubt even Jesus himself could exorcise."

"I can definitely relate to that," Emily said.

"Hey, enough with the dark side and all this talk of the past," I said. "Let's focus on the present."

Holding hands, we reclined on the windshield and studied the constellations for a while.

"I like it here," Emily said.

"Me, too," I agreed. And I meant it like I'd never meant anything before.

I leaned in close and kissed Emily, softly, first on the eyes, then the scar on her cheek, and finally her lips. I lingered there, and she and I made love beneath the stars on the hood of that Ford Bronco.

I found Emily kneeling over the toilet in a bathroom on the third floor of the band's Nashville mansion. She was sobbing and vomiting at the same time.

"Baby, what's wrong?" Panicked, I rushed to her and wrapped my arms around her.

"I'm sick," she said, leaning back against me. "And I'm no good. I know you love me, Brunky, but I'm just not a good person."

"What are you talking about? Of course you're good," I said. "You're an incredible, beautiful person."

She shook her head emphatically. "No, I'm not. You don't really know me, the deep down me."

She was obviously wasted and I spotted pill bottles in the floor nearby. "Hey, did you take all these?" I asked, my fear jumping up several notches. "How many did you take? Tell me."

"I took some...all of them, I guess...but I...I threw them back up," Emily said haltingly. "I got...I got scared. But I'll be okay...really I will."

"Maybe I should take you to the hospital...just to be safe. Don't you think--"

"No. No doctors," she said firmly, harshly. "I told you...I'll be okay."

Salty tears dropped off her cheeks, fell onto her bare feet, and made glistening trails along her ivory skin. I helped her to the bed, covered her gently with a blanket, and wished I could heal the hurting, fragile, little girl inside my lover.

15

I dreamed I was standing by my mother's coffin, staring down at the lifeless form of the woman who had carried me in her womb for days beyond her due date. In life, she had often berated me for this, attempting to teach me the terrors of tardiness, reminding me that my failure to come forth into the world in a timely manner brought upon her additional hours of misery, during which time she had cursed me and wished me out of her body.

In my dream, I, the Pupil, gazed upon the dead, delicate features of my Teacher, her pâté skin having been kneaded and plied by the skillful hands of the mortician, with rouge and blush meticulously applied by the funeral home's dutiful makeup artist. Her lips had been forced and sewn into an expression intended to display dignified solemnity, but to me, something between a sanctified sneer and a gleeful grimace still tittered uneasily upon the lips of the corpse in the casket. I twisted and groaned in my sleep, hands clenching and unclenching as it unfolded in my burning brain.

"Doesn't she look natural?" a dream-world woman said as she peered into the coffin.

She looks hideous, I thought, but I gave the woman an appropriately solemn funeral nod, then stared blankly until she moved on and away, off to rejoin the herd of boorish mourners dabbing their eyes with tissue, softly murmuring about how nice the flowers were, how kind the funeral home attendants had been, and how the dead woman appeared so life-like.

I turned my dream-gaze back to the empty shell that had been my matriarchal monarch, and studied her in a clinical manner, peering closely at the wrinkled skin, upturned nose, and sharp chin of the yellowed face framed by locks of someone else's hair, having lost her own as a result of the cancer and radiation treatments.

Even with she in death reposed, I could not escape the intimidating power of my mother. I felt very small in her presence, convinced that in galactic terms, I truly *was* a tiny creature, not all that different from the tiny creatures that would soon consume her body, from within and from without. Sweat gleamed on my forehead and nestled damply in my armpits as I dreamed her innards becoming a smorgasbord of delight for microorganisms of all creeds and colors.

Mother's eyelids twitched once, then again. "No, no, that can't be," I mumbled, grinding my teeth in tortured sleep, my muscles taut with terror like barbed wire strung too tightly from post to post. Suddenly her eyes burst open like orbs of bloody pus and her clamped jaws broke forth with rage. She pulled me against her brutal bosom, her pungent breath on my neck. The stink of death bored and poured into my pores. I tried to step away but my legs were held firm, I and all creatures alike, captured by gravity's grip on this soaring sphere, with only humans taking ourselves far too seriously and our place in the great chain never quite seriously enough. I felt myself crumbling like the weakest cosmic link in the unfathomable, unquenchable longing of humankind, an endlessly exploding, broken-hearted supernova on our immediate and distant horizon.

The empty sockets of my mother's eyes stared me down. Her hollow mouth gaped at me, and her words kicked and dangled about in my head like the legs of a hanged man. *Come here, son. Come closer. Closer. Give me your hand. Touch me. Kiss me.*

I burst from my dream world, shooting straight up like a crazed corpse, my mind shaken and stirred like an overwrought, dirty martini, loose olives bumping about in my brain. Blood-shot eyes wide, I sat for eternal minutes in the darkness, sweat beads dancing on my forehead to the rhythm of my ragged breath in the silent pre-dawn air.

Clovis, New Mexico, was a small town built around a train depot that had once been a major stop on the Santa Fe Railroad. It was flat and barren with adobe homes, dirt lawns, few trees, rocky peaks in the distance and a sky as big as the federal deficit. Main Street ran east-west directly through the center of town, a powerful line of demarcation with poverty to the south and affluence on the north side.

Emily and I sat on a bench in the afternoon sun and watched the trains pushing and pulling flatbeds, hoppers and tankers. Locals, hobos and tourists wandered about, mixing uneasily, keeping America as it has always been – the epitome of jagged juxtaposition, the jaded with the jolly. Children dashed about, getting their good clothes dirty, drinking sodas, wanting ice cream, asking their parents when they could ride the train, and posing for pictures that would fill family albums someday. Other children, generations hence, would peruse those albums and point to those pictures and ask, "Was that you, grandma, when you were a little girl?"

Chance and the strong scent of peppermint tugged us into a small curio shop owned and operated by Arthur and Merlina Hotchkiss. They were in their eighties and had been married for sixty-two years, all of them in Clovis, New Mexico.

"Sixty-two years," Arthur said. "Now I'm not sayin' they was all easy years, no sir, but they been good, all in all. We've had to work hard all our lives--"

"We had cattle," Merlina said proudly. "A hundred head, sometimes more."

Their conversation flowed smoothly between them like a well-practiced routine, and was comfortable as a warm quilt.

"And we growed sorghum," Arthur said. "Made a good livin' with it. I ain't sayin' it was easy, 'cause it sure 'nuff weren't. But a man's got to work for what he gets. Seems like some folks forgettin' that in this country, now ain't that the truth."

"We're retired now, really. We just piddle around here in the shop…keeps us busy. We can't bear to sit still," Merlina said, absently rearranging stacks of peppermint sticks and bowls of butterscotch drops on a counter.

Arthur added, "And we get to meet plenty of interesting people from all over, like you folks."

"Will Rogers was here once't a time," Merlina said. "I heard him give a little talk right down at the hotel, yes I did. Shook his hand too…this here one right here." She held it up for us to inspect. "He sure was something mighty special."

"Oh, don't start goin' on about Will Rogers," Arthur protested, as he winked at us. "I think she'd a' left me for Mr. Rogers if she'd had half a chance."

Merlina made a clucking sound and gave him a playful smack on the arm. "Oh, you and your foolishness," she said, then leaned in close to us and whispered, "I never could'a rode off with Mr. Will Rogers…I'm allergic to horses."

With that, they both laughed like second graders watching Saturday morning cartoons.

With the band on brief hiatus, Emily and I crossed into Texas where nothing changed but the road. Rather than north toward Amarillo or south for Lubbock, we stayed dead east on Route 145, a lonely, sunbaked, two-lane that shot off toward the horizon straight as the arrow of God.

"Think we'll end up like that old couple in Clovis?" Emily asked.

"What? Running a curio shop?" I kidded her.

Emily laughed, locked her arms around me and put her head against my chest as we blew past Lazbuddie.

That evening, somewhere in the high plains of north Texas, we sat with our cooler at dusk, and feasted on a bounty of cold beer and bologna sandwiches – thick deli slices on fresh white bread.

We were happy.

For a long while that night, in supreme silence and superlative solitude, we stretched out on our backs, pressed full against the cool earth, and watched the glimmering procession of stars, cosmic debris from an ancient detonation racing away from us.

The twisted dreams won't stop. They squeeze and pound my brain like an angry wash woman doing laundry on the rocks.

I dreamed I was making love to Emily. She was on top of me, riding me, grinding me slowly. I was moving with her, deep inside her warmth. She held my hands above my head, pinning me, and put her moist lips upon my mouth. Her soft, pink tongue swirled slowly with mine, and then licked the length of me. Her midnight tresses fell about my face, her jade eyes locked with mine as she moved upon me. She was wet and slick as she slid me toward the perfect moment.

Suddenly, a beastly creature pulled her from me and put his mouth upon hers. She tried to scream but her cries were muffled beneath him as he slid two fingers, then three, then four inside her and pumped. Then her threw her like a rag doll, face down on the bed beside me, and rode her from behind like an animal. He wore the Devil's grin as Emily screamed out in pain and lust and pleasure and fear.

I was unable to move, couldn't stop what was happening, trapped on the bed, my hands still above my head, held there, pinned there by someone else. Trying not to see the horror, I closed my eyes so fiercely that tears and blood trickled from the corners.

"You know you want it," a ghostly voice said. *"You know you do."* I opened my eyes to see my mother upon me, riding me now. She bent close and her breath was

cold and damp as she whispered in my ear, "*You killed me. You want me. You killed me.*"

I woke from my dream of terror and stumbled outside. My bile was vile and my vomit voracious, eager to explode upon the earth. I tripped and fell face-first into my own bloody regurgitation. Gravel, glass and pavement tore my cheeks and forehead, and I sobbed with the sorrow of the ages.

Emily and I were having a quiet – or at least, it started quietly – breakfast at a Denny's Restaurant somewhere in Arizona. I was musing about existentialism, seeking signs in the bottom of my cup. The waitress was a welcome sight as she warmed my coffee and the cockles of my heart. I stared at her and wondered, *What are cockles?* Apparently, mine are connected to my groin area.

The waitress' name was Anna Ray. "That's very pretty," Emily said. "I've never heard it before."

"I was named after my grandmother Anna. The middle name, Ray, was just something my mother came up with on the spur of the moment because she said I was like a beautiful ray of sunlight." Anna Ray beamed as she spoke.

"What a beautiful story," I said. "Your mother has keen insight."

"Yes, but she's a drunk," Anna Ray said matter-of-factly, and the sunlight disappeared from her face just as suddenly as it had appeared. She moved away quickly to serve other customers.

An elderly woman at the table beside us struck up a conversation. Her hair was white as virgin snow and it stood up in stiff spikes on her head as though she'd stuck her finger in an electrical socket and lived to tell of it. Her name was Dee, and she claimed to be an artist, a writer, a shaman, a traveler, an Avon saleslady, and, above all else, Chief Ambassador for her coven.

She scooted her chair to our table and spoke of life and death, and the wonders of the Spirit and the Dark Side. Gripping our hands tightly, she closed her eyes and trembled as she whispered, "The wreckage of life is sad and tragic, but often the healing is in the wreckage. I see much love in your young hearts, but life is a long road, a very long road. You will weave into, and eventually away from each other...but you will find each other again."

Emily was wide-eyed and shaking as she spoke with a strained voice, "Brunky, let's go. Please, I want to go now."

"Oh, my dear, young sweetie," Dee said, cupping Emily's face in her hands. "You are most precious, most precious. Let not your heart be troubled. All things will be clear in the end. Every debt will be paid."

As if on cue, the waitress returned with our bill.

Uncle Murphy, my dad's brother, lived in Fruita, New Mexico, and Emily and I stopped to visit. He looked like a tall Yosemite Sam, complete with red handlebar moustache and a long, unkempt beard. Uncle Murph was 70 years old, but he still drove an eighteen-wheeler for a living, and did much of his talking on a CB radio. Emily was spell-bound as he regaled us with stories – many of which I'd heard as a kid – of life on the road from Kennebunkport to the Klondike, from Cocoa Beach to Coronado Island.

"Boy, I sure do miss the old days," Uncle Murphy said. "But ya cain't throw an anchor out on time."

"What's the scariest thing that ever happened to you out on the road?" Emily asked. "You must have had some close calls."

"Well, they was this one time my rig blew a tire right at the top of Sandstone Mountain, steepest grade east of the Rockies, seven percent for seven miles. That ain't no sunny day. So, anyways, this tire blows and I says to myself, 'Hell, one monkey don't stop no show'. Wouldn't you know, another tire blows, just like that. Then this damn gear jammer with a lot lizard on his brain blew by me doin' at least eighty. Fool goin' eighty down Sandstone - can you imagine that?"

Emily shook her head no and asked, "What happened next?"

"Well, we're rollin' side by side down the mountain, see, and we come up on a damn pallet smack dab in the

26

middle the road. Wadn't nothin' I could do but hit it. One tire blew right away like a gunshot. You ever hear a gunshot up close?"

Emily shook her head yes. "My daddy shot the TV once. It was really loud."

Uncle Murphy raised an eyebrow at that and studied Emily.

"Because of a ballgame," Emily continued nervously. "I think he lost a bet."

"So, what happened on Sandstone Mountain, Uncle Murph?" I asked.

Uncle Murphy jumped back into his story. "Well, I hit that pallet and lose two more tires in an instant. Now I'm down four wheels and they was alligator skins all over that damn road. I tried to hold her straight but she was swingin' on me and I was bearin' down on a bug. So I had to put her off on the shoulder. Turned over and the whole damn thing tore apart and caught on fire."

"Wow," Emily said.

"Yeah, and the funny thing is, I was haulin' a load of poultry. And I do mean a shit-load of poultry."

"Wow," Emily repeated.

"Musta' been five thousand chickens. Half of 'ums dead and the other half's runnin' 'round this way and that, and a million feathers floatin' in the air. And with that fire burnin' strong they was fried chicken as far as the eye could see. Damn, it sure smelled good. If that ain't so, then there ain't a cow in Texas."

As we left Uncle Murphy that day, he took me aside for a moment and said, "That's a good one ya got there, boy. She's a sweet thing, a damn fine girl. Don't you lose her."

I crept to the edge of the bed where Emily lay bundled with the blankets pulled up almost entirely over her head. She seemed so still and lifeless that it frightened me for a moment. I woke her gently, carefully pulling the covers down a bit from her face.

"Emily, are you okay?" I said. "Emily, baby, can you hear me?"

Her eyes opened but her face was blank. She mumbled, "Goddess screaming in the jars of purple honey. I don't want to, I don't want to."

"Baby, wake up," I said. "You're dreaming."

"Daddy says…Daddy says…I'm a big girl now," she continued, muttering in a drugged dream state. "I wanna ride my bike…I wanna ride…but daddy won't let me. I'll be a big girl…big girl now…for daddy."

Feeling frightened and helpless, I caressed Emily's cheek and was smitten once again by her pure, simple beauty. I kissed her softly on the forehead, only inches from where twisted neurotransmitters tortured the one and only love of my life.

My dreams became ever more outrageous, as if to keep pace with Emily's. It was almost as though she and I were unknowingly waging some sort of unspoken dream war, each of us attempting to outdo the other in absurdity.

I dreamt Emily and I were running through city streets littered with bodies. Helicopters and small planes buzzed overhead. A phone rang constantly. There were French fries on the table. Raucous crowds marched across the land as an empire crumbled. I tried to wake from my nightmare, but could not, and went tumbling down reckless corridors where sleep hands groped me like monsters in a haunted house.

Then I dreamed that Emily and I were young teenagers, so very naive and in love. In my dreamscape, we were like twin souls, brother and sister, yet lovers of great renown. Our lives soared from black and white into a fantastical panorama of brilliant color, like something from *The Wizard of Oz*.

We went sailing the ocean, taking a voyage around the world until the skies turned black and great waves crashed over us. My mother came rushing out of the darkness and fell upon us like a great vulture upon rotting flesh. She slashed Emily's throat and cast her overboard. I watched my lover falling, bleeding, drowning, swirling round and round in the sea as it drained out a hole at the bottom of the ocean floor, like water going down a bathtub drain. I screamed in my dream and woke with a start, shooting straight up like a corpse shot forth from a coffin, trembling and sweating.

"Are you okay?" Emily whispered.

"Yeah, yeah, I think so," I mumbled. "I was dreaming...weird, scary dreams. Seems like I've had a lot of them lately."

"Yeah, me too."

I lay back for a moment to gather myself, and Emily snuggled up against me, her head on my chest. The sky outside was grim and grey with low clouds marching off to war, and rain gently pelting the window pane.

"Wonder what time it is," I said.

"It's about eight," Emily answered.

"Morning or evening?"

Emily laughed, "Morning, dear."

"I have to leave, you know," I said. "I have that meeting..."

"I know. I'm sorry I can't go with you."

"I'll be back tomorrow. Will you be okay?"

Emily nodded.

I pulled her close and kissed her for real, hard and deep. She moved her lithe body against mine. Her skin was warm like sunshine and her fingers trembled as they traced lines along my face. Then, mouth to mouth, we breathed into one another and her eyes opened wide with the innocent wonder of love.

"Maybe while I'm gone, you can look around for a place you like, something in our price range," I suggested. "And as soon as I get back, I promise we'll move out of here."

Emily looked worried.

"Is something wrong?" I asked.

She hugged her knees up tight against her chest, and said, "No, nothing. Nothing's wrong."

Cloudlike images mutter in my head,
Metal fingers lift my backbone from bed,
Melancholy headlines black my eye,
Say hello to the big goodbye,
Say hello to the big goodbye...

-- Michael Crisp

I slipped silently into our bedroom on the third floor, and quickly undressed. There was an odd odor in the room, but I was too tired to think about it. Emily was in bed, snuggled under the covers, only the top of her head visible. I slid under the blankets and pressed my naked body against hers, to spoon her from behind.

The moment I touched her, I knew something was wrong. I jerked the covers back and saw that she'd thrown up on the sheets. Fear gripped me and I whispered frantically, "Emily, Emily, Emily."

I rolled her over as gently as I could. Her face had a blank look...like the spaces of a crossword puzzle you can't solve. There was an empty prescription bottle clutched in each of her cold hands.

I couldn't speak. I didn't cry. I was numb. I was thinking only about how I couldn't seem to think. It was an eternal moment as though the waves of time were stuttering on frigid lips.

It's happening again, just like with my mother.
I lost my mind.

There was vomit on Emily's face, and her thighs and buttocks were soiled. I couldn't bear to see her that way, and I didn't want anyone else to. Quickly, I bathed her with warm soapy water and towels from our private bath, washing and drying every part of her beautiful body, lavishing her with tender care. I kissed her cold lips and stroked her as my lover. Temporary insanity ruled in the wake of my permanent loss; and in my disjointed mind I was seeing her as she *had been*, not as she now was.

I, the madman, moved my fingertips in tiny circles, caressing her as I had so many times before along thighs so smooth and girlish, buttocks so round and firm. I slid my fingers to the warmest place I'd ever known, the only place I'd ever truly called home. I wanted to hear that familiar moan, hear her purring softly like a kitten as I stroked her. But there was nothing. She was cold, dead, gone.

I pulled my hand away abruptly; horribly ashamed when I realized what I was doing. Tears welled up and streamed down my face as I rocked back and forth on the edge of bed. An hour passed, maybe two. My heart was numb and my brain was shattered. Or maybe it was the other way around. I couldn't tell.

A helicopter buzzed close to the house and brought me out of my daze. I called 9-1-1, reported a suicide, clutched Emily's cold body to my chest, and wept.

Chance and fury pushed me to the Whiskey Kitchen on Demonbreun Street in downtown Nashville. I drank enough to fell a lesser man and stared out the window, across the alleyway at a warehouse whose wares had long ago given up the ghost. The building's old bricks rose to meet the sky and the contrast was startling, so startling that I wept, right there in my booth.

"What's the matter, sweetie?" a smoky-eyed waitress asked.

"Brick to sky makes me cry," I said, pointing out the window. "See there where the baked red wall stands framed against bursting blue, unyielding blocks stacked up to fluid firmament?"

Nervously, the waitress bent down a bit and looked out the window toward where I pointed. "Uh, huh," she said slowly. "Of course, yes, sweetie. I see it." Then she backed away carefully.

I threw down another double shot of vodka, chased it with a full mug of beer, and scanned the barroom. There were scores of men in designer suits cutting deals over rum and coke, a big-breasted blonde in a too-tight blouse slipping outside for a smoke, a petite waitress with weary eyes laughing at a big tipper's unfunny joke, and a raging alcoholic in denial ordering eggs Benedict with no yoke.

I drank myself to the perfect drunk, an unrivaled state of inebriation so exquisite that I might still feel it years later. I dredged up a snoot-full of youthful memories, as though I was a very old man, drunk again on beers from the past, potent alcohol intricately intertwined with intense recollections, taking me back to when I was truly young, well-hung, and strung out on the dung of society's platter. I remembered the time I found Jesus. Or he found me. Or perhaps we staggered unintentionally into each other, knocking knees in the hallway when one of us was heading toward the bathroom, the other away from it. Can salvation be found in a chance encounter on the way to taking a leak? All I know is that I lugged my Jesus junk around in the trunk of my soul for years, like tattered garbage bags of ragged clothing destined for Salvation Army bins.

And so I reminisced there in my booth at the Whiskey Kitchen, loath to return to the present, the present where Emily was dead. In my head, I went back to my teenage years when I had no cares, back to when Pink Floyd surrounded me, pouring forth in massive waves from the 8-track player in my battered 1970 Plymouth Fury. Four doors, four wheels, and a million memories.

The waitress with the smoky eyes approached my booth again and spoke, but I did not see or hear. Cautiously, she put a hand upon my shoulder and suggested I have a cup of coffee or a glass of water.

Even though I was a patron in her establishment, I could not muster even one single patronizing smile. I looked hard at her with all the sorrow of my soul and said, "There is no coffee strong enough or water holy enough to cure what ails me."

34

For the next twenty-four hours I drank and wandered the streets of Nashville, a landscape littered with legions of leeches and lepers. I let myself be swept along the sidewalks, caught up in a blend of vacationers and locals in ten-gallon cowboy hats and expensive western boots, with expansive guts hanging over huge, shiny belt buckles. From bar to bar I drifted and allowed the live music to shake my elemental quarks like a cosmic kaleidoscope, hoping it would simply batter me into oblivion.

Shortly before dawn, I ended up on First Avenue, down by the Cumberland River, hanging out with the homeless. I cried like an honest-to-God, old-fashioned drunk. Snot and tears mixed and smeared on my face, and I rambled incoherently: *Why isn't life fair? Why do people have to die? Why do we keep secrets? Damn, I have to take a leak. Where is my car? I see demons. I want another barbeque. How do they make glass out of sand? Why do people die? Where the hell is my car?*

None of the hobos had answers, but one of them put his arm around me warmly and cried with me. He gave me a piece of moldy bread and I ate it. And there we sat, two downtrodden disciples of disappointment, breaking bread together, and worshipping the lord of losers.

"I really didn't know her very long," I mumbled. "We should have had more time together. It's not fair."

"Some things in life," the hobo said. "Don't make no damn sense at all."

35

I did not want to attend Emily's funeral, but I was willing myself to go, steeling myself against what was to come, billing myself for long overdue debts of the soul. Between the vodka and the sorrow, I was floating somewhere in the cloudy skies of misery, stumbling down the trail of disillusionment, and lost in the land of I-Don't-Give-A-Damn.

Emily's parents, long ago divorced, had come together to make the funeral arrangements. I'd never met them until that day, and they were nothing like I imagined. Their faces were lined with years of worry, sallow with regret. They seemed genuinely distraught by the loss of their daughter, in spite of the things Emily had told me about them and her relationship with them. The mother was an older image of Emily – the resemblance astounding – with the same dimples, weepy eyes and thick hair. *That's exactly what she would've looked like*, I thought. *Only happier. I could have made Emily so very happy.*

While they spoke with the mortuary staff, I moved about like a zombie, shook hands like a fish, nodded appropriately like a bobble-head doll, and agreed with whatever was suggested. When the opportunity presented itself, I slipped away to join the hillbilly smokers outside and bummed a cigarette.

When the visitation services began, I sat in the back of the viewing room, slumped in my seat, trying not to see or speak to anyone, sipping surreptitiously from the flask in my pocket. Tugging absently on my goat chin hair, I thought about my mother, and dark shadows pitched across my eyes like unkempt bangs cut by a brutal barber. I'd been right there at her side when she decided to die, decided she could bear no more, and I became her unwitting accomplice, as she simply shut her eyes and silently surrendered. Then there were no more crises in the night. No more chemotherapy brutalization or radiation rigors. No more hemoglobin conversations or white blood cell supplementations. No more injections, pills, morphine drips, nurses' rigid instructions, doctors' somber speeches, or sadly beeping monitors in the hushed, disinfectant-permeated hospital nights.

I despised my mother for giving up the ghost, but even more so for pulling me down with her, ensnaring me in an everlasting web woven with strands of guilt and fibers of fury. I remembered how my family wavered that day in the white-tiled hall of the hospital with muffled sobs, awkward embraces, and whispers of grief. Aunt Kathryn played her role as ambassador for Christ in the family's time of need, and urged us all to rejoice that mother was now safe in the loving arms of Jesus, at peace in the bosom of the heavenly father.

But my father knew nothing of peace, and he spit his words out like snuff scraps, "If there is a God, he's a vicious bastard." Cursing God was as close to God as my father would ever be.

I sifted through these memories as the mourners moved about me in small herds, murmuring condolences, commenting on the flowers. Against the back of my brain, upon my pons projector, I replayed my mother's final services – the interminable wake, the intolerable funeral led by a droning Baptist preacher, and the god-awful, grave-side ceremony with the congregation plodding through melancholy hymns intended to celebrate my mother's joyous entrance into the indescribable glory of her heavenly home. The irony, as well as the truth of her death, was lost on everyone but me, and I refused to sing. All of it seemed such a long time ago, and the continents of my life had shifted to a fault on tragic tectonic plates.

"Brunky, Brunky," someone was saying. "Are you okay?" A woman placed her hand gently on my shoulder and I gazed up vacantly. "It's me, Dena, from high school," she said. "Don't you remember me?"

"Yes, I remember," I said slowly. "I remember too much." Dena's sweet smile cut across the years, back to a time when things were so much simpler. Or at least they seemed to be.

Something out of the ordinary was happening at the front of the viewing room and it caught my attention. Two tabloid photographers were poised over Emily's coffin, taking pictures of her because of her connection to me and the band. I learned later that Emily's seemingly benign parents had been willing and able to exploit their only daughter's death for ten thousand dollars. They could've gotten so much more than that, and their ignorance simply confirmed that they truly were stupid white trash.

I moved quickly through the crowd and took the pair of photographers by surprise. I slammed one man's head down hard against the closed, bottom half of the casket; and threw the other man into a beautiful standing spray of lilies, gladiolas and roses. I could've sworn I saw Emily smile. I leaned over her corpse, lightly kissed her lifeless lips, and gently traced one finger along the faint scar on her cheek.

It's our scars that make us what we are.

After being thrown out of the funeral services, I wandered the familiar streets of my boyhood home, Beckley, West Virginia, for hours before going back to my hotel. In my room I sucked on my vodka bottle like a newborn sucks on the teat. Thinking of what I'd lost, I spilled tears on my guitar, wrote a song and wailed it to the four walls of my room.

That sky, those clouds,
Remind me of a picture,
That used to hang in our living room,
Said that Jesus was coming soon,
Kinda silver, orange and blue,
So damn pretty, it can't be true,
I get all mixed up in my head,
Trying to remember the things you said,
Bye, bye……baby, bye, bye…

If you ever had a big freight train
Rolling through your heart,
Then maybe you know how it feels
When the nightmares start,
If you run from the light long enough
Sooner or later, it's bound to get dark,
Maybe it's time for a change,
Could be you missed your mark,
Bye, bye……baby, bye, bye…

God ain't some big sugar daddy,
He that has ears, let him hear,
Sometimes when you hurt the most
Is when things become all too clear,
Off in the distance, hear the sound
Of cold hard cash striking the ground,
Somebody got a soul to sell,
A little piece of heaven on the streets of hell,
Bye, bye......baby, bye, bye...

It's not that I'm disgusted,
I'm just sick of the whole damn thing,
Sitting here alone and busted,
Staring at this diamond ring,
They say you learn from the hard times,
Then I should be one smart motherfucker,
Why do I believe the things you say?
I'm either a fool or a sucker,
Bye, bye......baby, bye, bye...
Bye, bye......baby, bye, bye...

I quit the band. Nobody was happy about my decision.

The lead singer warned me, "You're making the biggest mistake of your life." The drummer chimed in, "Mate, you'll see us rocking on the telly, and running out and about scoring hash and hitting strange all over God's creation, and then you'll be one sorry-ass bloke." And our manager played the guilt angle. "We can't replace you, Brunky," he said. "You're letting every single one of us down, putting us in a real bind."

"Sorry, but I'm in a real bind of my own," I said. "Besides, you guys will be fine. I mean, come on, it's really not that hard to find another guitar player who can sing harmonies."

But they were still pissed, and so was I. They were forgetting how many times I'd been the only glue holding the band together, how many times I'd covered for each of them when they got themselves into some sort of bullshit situation, and how often I'd made the right connections and decisions to bring us the success we'd had up to that point.

As they continued to protest and plead, I shook my head and walked out the door. The band can be a story for another day.

August 28, 1977

I'd retired from serious drinking at age twenty-five, just before I met Emily, but I decided it was time to go back to work in my original field of choice. I rededicated myself to a career in alcoholism, applied myself fully, and put in long hours burning the midnight booze. I had about six thousand dollars in cash remaining; I figured I'd see how long it would last. After that, I didn't know what I'd do. And I didn't care.

I stocked up on vodka and spent more than a month secluded in the Holiday Inn, playing guitar, flipping channels on the television, speaking to no one but myself, and drinking excessively. I routinely refused housekeeping services. I didn't shower or shave, and the long strands of my goat chin goatee were soon accompanied by a full beard.

When hunger gnawed at my stomach strongly enough for me to take notice, I slipped down to the complimentary continental breakfast for a bagel or raided the vending machine. Once I ordered a pizza and when I paid the delivery guy, he said, "Hey, aren't you that guitar player—" But before he could finish his question, I screamed *No!* and threw the pizza at him. After he was gone, I picked it up off the floor and ate it – hair, dirt and all.

No one knew where I was – I had cut myself off from the music business and the rest of the world. I was in a tenuous position on the tightrope of life, and in no condition to deal with any more bullshit.

I deteriorated, disintegrated, and desolated like cheap toilet paper at the bottom of a truck stop commode. My thoughts tumbled like socks in a dryer. All my parts of speech were in the past tense and all my participles were dangling like a dead man at the end of a rope.

September 2, 1977

I wandered into the 7-11 and a man tried to tell me about Jesus as we stood near the counter-top oven where hot dogs rotated in all their naked glory and were not ashamed. The man said that Jesus loved me and had a master plan for my life. He said that all things work together for good for them that love God. I should have been kind, should have been tolerant, could have said *No thanks, I'm not interested*, or I simply could have said nothing at all. But I did none of those things. Instead I unleashed a torrent from my sick soul.

I faced the man and ranted, "I am sick of people who try to put a positive spin on everything. They talk about a universal plan, the will of God, or some other bullshit. You ever notice that there's always that one guy that gets interviewed on TV who survives a disaster of some type - a plane crash, flood, fire, or whatever misery God heaped upon man that particular day – and the man tells how hard he prayed, and how God is such a good and loving God, how God answers prayer, and how God saved him from death? Really, buddy? Is that how it works? *Really?*"

I was poking the man in the chest now, over and over again with each sentence. "So God kills 127 people in a plane crash, but he hears and answers the prayer of this one jerk, and saves him. You don't think any of those other people were praying too? Was that guy just the only one that God really loved? It's all bullshit. Accept the obvious – life sucks. It's full of random and chaotic heartache and loss, and all the positive thinking in the world won't change that reality. You can splash a turd with cologne, wrap it up in fine linen, and put a bow on it, but it's still a stinking turd."

The man put his hand kindly upon my shoulder and said, "My friend, Jesus understands what you're going through. He can wash away all your wickedness. He will forgive your sins and your unbelief."

"Oh, yeah?" I whispered, "Will he forgive this?" And then I struck the man in the face with my fist. I don't know exactly why I did it, and I'm ashamed that I did it. It happened so quickly that it took me a moment to realize what I'd done. My life had been like an endless chain of sorrows for as long as I could remember, and it was as if that chain suddenly wrapped around my brain and squeezed out my sanity.

The man staggered backwards, surprised, but not nearly as surprised as I was. "I'm sorry, I'm sorry," I said, trembling with synaptic schisms. "I'm really not a violent person; I shouldn't have–"

And then the man hit me back. I suppose he believed that it was his responsibility to mete out the righteous judgment of God. His knuckles smashed into my jaw and I fell backward into a cardboard potato chip display. Bags of Ruffles, pretzels, and other assorted snacks crunched beneath me, and a busted bag of corn chips landed in my lap and spilled out on the floor. They reminded me of Emily and her corn chips. I began to cry – tears, snot, and blood falling onto Fritos.

September 13, 1977

Not long after the 7-11 fiasco, my relationship with The Holiday Inn was terminated when I smashed the window in my room with the floor lamp. After paying for the damages, I downsized and cut my daily costs by moving into the nearby Motel 6. They kept the light on for me but it didn't help; I was still shrouded in darkness.

I gazed out the window for days as a cold, thick fog hung in the West Virginia hills the way Emily's death hung in my heart.

I dyed my goat-chin hair a brilliant shade of blue, and I don't know why.

Time passed like a flash flood up a holler.

I'm spending money like a sieve, I said to myself.

That doesn't even make any sense, I answered back. *Sieves don't spend money.*

Sieves let things pass through, I said. *And that's what's happening to my money.*

It would make more sense to say I'm spending money like a Rockefeller, I suggested to myself.

You're drunk, I said.

Oh, I'm way past drunk, I answered.

Suddenly my mother's voice interrupted my conversation with a whisper from the back of my brain, "Money doesn't grow on trees, you know."

I was pacing the floor in my room when she spoke, and I stopped abruptly at the sound of her voice. My mother had been strangely silent for months, having withdrawn for a while as she sometimes did. For several long moments, I stood very still on the worn Berber carpet, waiting for her to speak again. But she did not.

Where are you?

Nothing.

I looked under the bed, in the closet, in the shower, out in the hall…but I could not find her.

Ted & Tessa

There was a knock on my door. Barefoot, shirtless, un-showered, unshaven, and uncertain, I was not in the mood for visitors. But this company was relentless.

"Come in! Just come the hell in," I yelled when I could bear no more knocking.

"I shall come in, by the by," a familiar voice said. "But the door is steadfastly locked."

I stumbled to the door and opened it. Ted W. Mills, my best friend in the world, was there with his arm around an interesting young woman who possessed one of those staggering smiles of glorious white teeth typically only seen on the face of a movie star. She was dressed completely in black – bell-bottom jeans, a *Ramones* tee shirt, a biker jacket, and combat boots.

"Hi, I'm Tessa. I'm with him," she said, pointing at Ted mischievously. "We're in love."

She hugged me tightly and warmly as though she'd known me forever. I looked over her shoulder at Ted, my eyes wide with surprise. Tessa leaned back from me a bit, still embracing me, and said, "Uh, you got a little something."

"Wh-what?" I murmured, a bit dumbstruck.

"Right there," she said, pointing. "There…you got something, uh, stuck…" Her voice trailed off.

I moved my hand slowly up to my face. There were pieces of pork rind and other snack food crumbs in the matted and ratty hair of my goat chin spike of beard.

"I am not touching you until you fully remove all debris from your beard," Ted said.

We smiled big at each other and embraced for a long time.

Ted and I met in junior high school, and although both of us were social misfits and outcasts, Teddy was most certainly cast out a bit farther than me. That common rejection was part of what bound us so tightly together. While some people mistakenly thought there might be hope for me in civilized society, no one ever held such illusions about Ted W. Mills. My father affectionately called him "the fucking oddest ball on the court;" but the truth is, had there been a gathering of oddballs, Ted would likely have been the odd man out.

Ted and I had bonded immediately, forming a friendship, a partnership that was scorned by our classmates and sometimes questioned by teachers, parents, and other "concerned" adults. We shared a love of philosophy, and as young teenagers we read the works of Socrates, Voltaire, and Kant, devouring them as hungry men eat meat and three. While our school mates attended dances and sporting events, we discussed Edna St. Vincent Millay, Ezra Pound, existentialism and predestination. While they sold candy bars door to door or held car washes to raise money for the school band, Ted and I drank liquor, smoked weed, and played guitar. We blazed our own outrageous trail and strayed always far from the beaten path.

"I heard about Emily," Ted said softly. "I know there's nothing I can say…except that I'm so very sorry. I know how much you loved her…and I loved her too. I wish I could've been here for you, been here for the funeral, but I didn't even know about her passing until they brought me out of the desert."

"I know," I said. "It's okay."

52

"I didn't know Emily," Tessa said, "But I'm very sorry for your loss."

"Thank you," I said. I took another swig of vodka. "What can you do…shit happens."

"There is one thing you could do – step away from the alcohol," Ted suggested. "How long has it been since you've eaten? Or showered?"

Ted looked at Tessa and said, "Trust me; he does not usually look quite this bad. Clean him up and he is actually a halfway decent looking fellow."

"I think he looks…" Tessa said, tilting her head to the side, trying to find the appropriate word to describe my filthy condition. "Um, rugged."

"Yes, indeed," Ted said, grinning. "Rugged."

"But, it is truly awesome to meet the famous Brunky, the man I've heard so much about," Tessa said, pushing the conversation in a more uplifting direction. "Ted Mills loves you very much, you know. And if Ted loves you, then I love you."

I had no glib answer for that. Tessa's mesmerizing smile and natural charm knocked me off my feet and left me bumbling for words. So I sat down on the bed.

"What are you doing here? Are you just on leave?" I asked after my head cleared.

"I am out; they have released me for good," Ted answered. "I returned home a few weeks ago."

"How did you find me?"

"The grapevine," Ted said. "And believe me, there were not many grapes on the vine. We have been sniffing your trail for weeks all over the southern half of the state. And, apparently, you got into some sort of pugilistic altercation at a convenience store. Is this true, Brunky?"

"Yeah, well, sorta," I answered sheepishly. "It was quite embarrassing."

"And you also busted up your room at the Holiday Inn," Ted said.

"Guilty," I said. "I just don't know what's wrong with me. I used to be in control of myself and felt like I could handle anything that came my way. But now...now it's like I'm losing my grip, like I'm teetering precariously on a very dangerous ledge."

"You can talk to me, Brunky. You know that," Ted said. "And if we talk it out, we will work through it. We always have, right?"

"I don't want to talk about it," I mumbled. "And I'm suddenly very tired of all this."

"This conversation?" Ted asked.

"No, this," I answered, looking around the room. "I'm tired of all...*this*."

"Perhaps you should come live with us and Uncle Jimmy for a while," Ted suggested.

"Yes, that's exactly what you'll do," Tessa interjected, jumping up. "Enough of this chit-chat. Come on, you're moving in with us."

"I am?"

"Of course you are," Tessa said. "We insist."

"Look, I'm just trying to figure some things out right now," I argued, refusing to stand up. "I need some more time to –"

"Nope." Tessa put a strong hand under my armpit and hoisted me to my feet. "You can't live here alone in your misery," she said. "You'll run out of money long before you run out of misery."

She was right about that.

"Okay." I said. And so I did.

My belongings were Spartan – Emily's diary, one suitcase, one backpack, one guitar – and we loaded them quickly into Ted's 1948 Studebaker Champion Regal DeLuxe 4-door tan sedan. From the back seat, I waved goodbye to the hotel phase of my life. I was now one unemployed, broken-hearted, guitar-playing, singer-songwriter bound for the backwoods Promised Land also known as Egeria, West Virginia. And as the three of us roared up and down mountains, and wound round pretzel curves and switchbacks not meant for the faint of stomach, I bemoaned my sorrows but smiled at my good fortune, now rescued by my comrade and his charming, uncommon companion.

Uncle Jimmy lived where coal was truly king, up a holler downwind from an abandoned tipple, in an upscale shack only slightly nicer than those of his neighbors. His humble abode, at the end of a dirt road, was twenty by twenty – four hundred square feet of claustrophobic country comfort – with running water *and* electricity.

"We livin' like pigs on bacon," Uncle Jimmy said as he embraced me, welcoming me to his home.

I hadn't seen Uncle Jimmy in nearly ten years, but he looked exactly the same as I remembered him. He was short and wiry, but with bulging, Popeye forearms, as though he'd just consumed a large can of spinach. His hair was scruffy and white like that of a billy goat; and, as always, there was a cigarette clinging precariously to his lower lip.

He was Ted's uncle, his father's older brother, but everyone who knew him called him Uncle Jimmy. As one might expect, Ted's father and Uncle Jimmy were a lot alike, especially regarding the large chip each carried on his shoulder. Neither was even remotely handsome, and they enjoyed large amounts of brown liquor and frequent fisticuffs. Both smoked cigarettes the way Jimi Hendrix played guitar, and there were no weak links in their smoking chain. And both hustled pool and couldn't pass a table without racking them up and taking some sorry sucker for all his money.

Uncle Jimmy had never concerned himself much with personal hygiene, hair styles, fashion, or political correctness. He had a disdain for the law and anyone in authority, and he considered it his personal mission to *knock down a few pegs anyone who was riding a high horse*, as he liked to say it. He could have been the poster boy for many a conspiracy theorist organization. During his brief stint in the military, Uncle Jimmy and Uncle Sam had not gotten along very well. He was crude and raw in speech and manner, but, unlike Ted's no-account, abusive father, Uncle Jimmy had a deep down good streak that ran close to his heart.

Uncle Jimmy generously let Ted and Tessa have the one, tiny bedroom while he slept on the couch; and I was assigned the cramped, slanted, utility room that leaned over on a stack of cinderblocks that was slowly settling into the earth. It was a far cry from the life I'd been living just a few months earlier in an 18,000 square foot mansion in Nashville, Tennessee, sleeping on Egyptian cotton, 1500 thread-count sheets in a king-sized bed with the love of my life. Now I was bunking on a busted futon that Uncle Jimmy had purchased years ago at a yard sale for five dollars. It gave me a four dollar sleep.

Snow started to fall as the four of us sat under an apple tree and drank beer. Between the flakes, I stole furtive glances at Ted's intriguing girlfriend. Her eyes were dark and mysterious like the back water in the channels below Shippingport, Pennsylvania; and her hair was bleached platinum blonde, cropped short and spiked like the punk rockers just coming out of England.

Tessa had been born and raised in the mountains of West Virginia, though she was anything but a typical Appalachian girl. Her parents were authentic old-school hippies, and firm believers in the earth-grain, minimalistic, protect-the-environment, grow-your-own-weed frame of mind.

From what I could tell, she rarely shaved under her arms. She had numerous piercings with studs in her ears, nose, tongue, and belly button, and a variety of colorful tattoos, none of which were *Mother*. She was eager to show them off – a revolver made of bones tattooed on her thigh, a Celtic knot on her back, and a splash of stars that flowed up the right side of her neck and onto her scalp beneath her blonde hair.

"Didn't all those piercings and tattoos hurt?" I asked.

"Most of them not really," Tessa replied. "The tongue hurt some, but the one down below was the worst."

"Down below?"

"My inner labia," she said.

"Ah," I said, raising my eyebrows.

"It is there, my friend," Ted said with a grin. "I have made visual confirmation."

"I'm not big on flash art, but I allowed myself the stars," Tessa said. "The knot and the revolver are for sure unique. No one else in the world has one like them."

"How do you know?" I asked.

"Because I knew the artist. They were very personal to him, unique designs of his own given only to me."

"Sounds as though I should be jealous of this tattoo fellow," Ted said.

"Dahling, you have nothing to fear," Tessa swooned with maudlin flair. "For I love only you." She kissed him on the lips, they rolled in the snowy grass, and I studied the sky for meteors.

Christmas dinner was fried potatoes and deer meat that Uncle Jimmy sizzled with bourbon in a cast iron skillet. Our gift exchange was meager, but it's the thought that counts. Uncle Jimmy gave me one of his old pistols, a .45 caliber Remington wrapped in a brown paper bag. "Ya never know when you're gonna need a good gun, and I mean a *real* one," he said, by way of explanation. "Not like that little .22 Beretta you got."

Tessa gave Uncle Jimmy a carton of Marlboros and me a six-pack of tube socks with a big red bow. To Ted she gave a full night of passionate, rowdy love-making. I would have gladly traded my socks for what he got.

In truth, Ted and Tessa regularly rocked the small house with the rhythm of love, knocking the bed railing against the wall with a steady clacking sound that reminded me of a train's steel wheels passing over the rail connectors on a track. Tessa often quoted Proust and Rimbaud during their copulation experimentations. Uncle Jimmy and I tried not to hear, but we couldn't help it. She half sang, half moaned, "surrounded by streaming shadows, I rhymed aloud, and as if they were lyres, plucked the laces of my wounded shoes, one foot beneath my heart." French poetry apparently drove Ted wild, or at least, the way Tessa did it. I'd learned something new about my best friend, something I didn't necessarily want to know.

I wandered in the cold woods for hours, just as I had every other day of the new year. I collected acorns by the hundreds and threw them at squirrels, but the squirrels simply considered the tiny missiles to be friendly fire. I sat for a while on a rock and watched the elm and chestnut trees battle for forest supremacy. I listened to the wind, wrote poetry, and felt like Thoreau. When I grew weary of that, I conducted target practice in an adjacent holler with my Christmas gift, the Remington pistol, and felt like Teddy Roosevelt.

But I could not bring myself to read Emily's diary. I desperately wanted to, but for some reason, I still couldn't do it.

I revitalized my career in heavy drinking, though not quite as ferociously as I had during my hotel phase. I lay on the futon sipping vodka, and drifted away with music that tugged and tore at my soul. In addition to an 8-track player and a tape of Leo Sayer, Uncle Jimmy had a small turntable with headphones, and a glorious stash of old vinyl from the 1950's, 60's and 70's from which to choose.

I wept freely with the hiss and crack of albums like *The Freewheelin' Bob Dylan*, *Five Feet of Soul* by Jimmy Rushing, *Year of the Cat* by Al Stewart, Ivory Joe Hunter's *Since I Met You Baby*, and The Moody Blues' *Days of Future Passed*.

I put a lot of miles in a short time on Uncle Jimmy's old needle and turntable.

February in the mountains makes people do strange things.

After breakfast the four of us sat around the small metal dining table and sipped coffee laced with hard liquor. Uncle Jimmy blew rings of smoke up toward the bulb that dangled at the end of a cord sticking out of a hole in the ceiling where a light fixture used to be. A dog barked somewhere in the distance and a group of ugly crows landed out front and stalked arrogantly across the yard.

"Life's a bitch," I said matter-of-factly.

"Yep, sure is," Uncle Jimmy said. "Maybe it's time we took a drive, got the hell out of here."

"Let's do it! I need to see some things," Tessa said excitedly. "Do you guys realize that I've never even been west of the Mississippi?"

"Now, that is a shame. All the good shit's out west," Uncle Jimmy said. "And this country's goin' to hell fast so you better see it 'fore it's gone."

Seeing the rising tide around him, Ted knew there was no point resisting, even if he wanted to. "I suppose a road trip might help Brunky's state of mind," Ted said.

"What's wrong with my state of mind?" I asked.

"You are wallowing in a funk" Ted said. "We need to help you break the cycle, help you embrace the Now."

"I can wallow if I want," I said.

"The solution to your sorrow is as near as your intention, my friend," Ted said.

I smirked at Ted and said, "What is that supposed to mean?"

"You know exactly what it means. I do not aim to be insensitive or hurtful, Brunky, but it is time for you to let go of the past."

"Make me."

"How 'bout both of you shut the hell up and pack," Uncle Jimmy said.

And so we did.

We roared across county and state lines in Ted's tan Studebaker, our immediate destination the other side of the Mississippi. From there, we had no clue.

At first consideration, being on the road sounded like a good idea for my state of mind. But the longer I was trapped in the vehicle, the more time I had to reflect, and the more time for voices from the past to whisper in my ear. I discovered that my mother still had plenty to say to me, and Emily's voice was always there as well. Every mile of road that passed beneath the Studebaker's wheels seemed to bring me one step closer to some sort of dangerous, psycho-spiritual epiphany. I imagined myself being called to a higher purpose for the first time in my life.

By the evening of day one on the road, we stood beneath the Arch in St. Louis and peered across the Mississippi.

"There it is, Tessa," Ted said, his arms wrapped lovingly around her from behind.

"Let's do this," Uncle Jimmy said. "Let's cross this damn river so Tess can see what's on the other side."

The Studebaker groaned back to life and we leapt into Missouri like children into a mud puddle. Uncle Jimmy and Ted rotated the driving responsibilities and we rolled on all night long.

February 15, 1978

The sun came up and chased us down in the middle of Kansas. Weary of the Interstate and having achieved our initial goal – the other side of the Mississippi – we wandered back roads in the true spirit of adventure.

We got out of the car where a dirt road crossed a railroad track at perfect right angles. The road shot off straight into infinity, and the track into eternity, both ways as far as the eye could see. The wind blew hard across the level landscape, stirring up dirt devils, scattering seed, and pushing clouds across the sky like late-night shoppers being hurried out of a closing store.

"My god, it's so flat," Tessa said. "I've seen it in magazines and the movies but that doesn't do it justice. It's so beautiful it makes you believe in God."

"Beautiful? That's not the word I'd use," Uncle Jimmy said. "It's flat, is what it is."

"If we were in a combat situation," Ted observed. "We would be in a position of extreme vulnerability."

Tessa shook her head and chided him, "Well, we're not in combat now, are we?"

"No, we are not," Ted said, smiling and wrapping his arms around her. "I hereby proclaim a ceasefire."

And so we dozed peacefully for a few hours in the shade of a cottonwood tree beneath the smiling sun, with the good breeze tussling our hair and birds dancing in the branches of our minds.

February 19, 1978

We slept out on the high Colorado plains where the wind pushed gently through the tall grass, drifting and murmuring like a sad ghost. When I was certain the others were fast asleep, I removed Emily's diary quietly from my backpack, as I had so many other nights, and held it to my chest. The stars stayed steady above me, staring, watching, waiting to see what I would do.

Open it, I said to myself. *It's time.*

I opened the diary and began to read about myself by the bright light of the full moon. There would be no sleep for me that night.

I pored through the pages, feeling guilty and ashamed, like a crude voyeur peering in on the soul of a dead girl. But I pressed on, unable to restrain myself. *She was the love of my life*, I thought. *She would want me to read it. I must read it.*

The diary contained a wide variety of entries: mundane reports of daily chores and activities, descriptions of Emily's anxiety, pain and fear, and numerous passages of which I could make little sense. But my soul ran aground on a few select excerpts, perplexing passages filled with dark portent and no answers:

May 30: Men can be such pigs. Always groping, pushing, reaching where they have no business. Why is this guy pursuing me? Why won't he leave me alone?

July 11: Things are always so complicated. Why is love so hard? I wish there was someone I could turn to. I wish my mother cared for me. If only I could pick up the phone right now and ask her what I should do. But I can't. I have no one to turn to.

August 17: I wish I knew how to tell Brunky about all this. I'm so ashamed. He deserves better than me.

August 18: I feel so conflicted and confused. I do love Brunky so much, but there's a small part of me deep inside that wonders...

August 19: I feel as though I have now bartered with the Devil himself. Brunky was away again, and I couldn't seem to resist. Maybe I didn't want to. I don't know. I don't know anything anymore. God, help me, I don't want to hurt Brunky.

Too late.

When the sun rose in the morning, I was there waiting for it. Sitting in the Colorado grass, I toasted the sunrise with the last of my vodka. Truth had come to me on moonbeams in the night; rage would come by day. I was a changed man.

"What happened?" Ted asked, instantly picking up on my distress. "What's wrong with you?"

"What makes you think anything's wrong with me?"

"I can tell by the look on your face."

"You can't tell shit," I said.

"Are you drunk again?"

"No," I replied calmly. "I've just been up all night drinking."

Ted sat down in the grass beside me. "I do not like to see you this way. Talk to me, Brunky."

I stood up and staggered away. "Not right now," I mumbled. "Not yet."

"Come on, Brunky…" Ted pleaded.

"No," I said firmly. "I just need some time to think it all through."

"One day you may run out of time."

"I can take you, old man," Tessa said, part playful, part serious.

Uncle Jimmy rolled his eyes and said, "Bull—shit," in two very long, distinct syllables.

"You want to go?" Tessa said. "Let's you and me go, right here, right now."

"Oh, Tessa, pipe down," Ted said. "Don't get your dander up."

"*Pipe down? Dander?*" Tessa laughed. "What century are you from?" She turned back to Uncle Jimmy. "Come on, Uncle Jimmy. I bet I can pin you."

Uncle Jimmy shook his head dismissively. "No thanks, young lady."

"You don't think I can, do you? It's because I'm girl, isn't it?" Tessa said, pushing the issue.

"Well, yeah," Uncle Jimmy said. "If ya got to know the damn truth, it's because yer a girl. I ain't gonna kick no little girl's ass."

Tessa grabbed Uncle Jimmy's arm and twisted it quickly behind his back. Then she spun around and swept his legs out from under him, sending him sprawling on his butt.

"Goddamn it, Tess," Uncle Jimmy shouted. "I'm sixty-eight years old. What are ya tryin' to do, break my hip?"

Suddenly embarrassed by her actions, Tessa apologized, "Oh, God, I'm so sorry, Uncle Jimmy. I'm really *really* sorry. Sometimes I just get carried away. I can't stand it when someone thinks I can't do something just because I'm female. It really pisses me off."

"I see that," Uncle Jimmy said.

"And, oh my God, I had no idea you were *that old*," Tessa said as she reached down to help him up.

Uncle Jimmy took advantage of her unbalanced position. He grabbed her hand and pulled her face first to the ground beside him. She yelped as he twisted her arm behind her as she had done to him.

"Don't feel so damn good, does it?" Uncle Jimmy said.

In a flash, Tessa bent her legs up and back like a gymnast and wrapped them around Uncle Jimmy's neck, pulling his head down and contorting his body in a way that no sixty-eight year old body should ever be contorted.

He did not, however, release his grip on her arm. And though her impressive maneuver had greatly increased his pain, it also pulled her own arm even more tightly behind herself. They were twisted and intertwined like a human pretzel, both of them crying out, "Ow, ow, ow!"

"Let go of my arm!" Tessa said.

"Not till you let loose 'a my head," Uncle Jimmy fired back.

"We'll let go together," Tessa suggested. "On the count of three."

"Oh, no," Uncle Jimmy said. "How do I know you'll really let go? You're a sneaky little thing."

Laughing, Ted said, "Okay, you two. Break it up before someone really gets hurt."

"Teddy, make your girlfriend let go of my head," Uncle Jimmy shouted.

Ted pleaded, "Come on, Tessa, let go. Quit picking on Uncle Jimmy."

"I'm not going to be the one who gives in," Tessa said.

"You are both being childish," Ted said.

I pointed my pistol toward the sky and calmly pulled the trigger, not even sure if it was still loaded. It was.

Everyone screamed, including me. Both wrestlers released their grips and jumped to their feet.

"Holy Bejeezus!" Uncle Jimmy yelled. 'Are ya tryin' to give an old man a heart attack?"

"Why in God's name did you do that?" Ted shouted. "You were standing right behind me. Now my ears are ringing and I cannot hear."

"Worked, didn't it?" I said smugly.

Ted cupped a hand to his ear and yelled, "What?"

Ted's grand and royal 1948 Studebaker gave up the ghost somewhere north of the Four Corners area. There was no ceremony or warning; it simply sat down on the side of a lonely road and refused to go another mile. Uncle Jimmy and Ted tinkered with its innards, clanging tools on metal, cursing the heat, and wiping sweat from their brows, but when all was said and done, we were forced to do the red dirt walk.

We studied the map and strapped on our backpacks, loaded with as many necessities as we could carry. Uncle Jimmy was immediately delighted with the new direction our adventure was taking, but Ted and Tessa were less enthusiastic about the situation. As for me, I was fully reconciled to the harsh reality and was not afraid or at all concerned with this turn of events.

"Brunky, what about your guitar?" Tessa shouted from the car.

"I don't need it anymore," I answered and kept walking.

"But isn't it worth a lot of money?" Tessa asked.

"I don't care," I said.

There come rare moments in a man's life when he seems to cross some personal continental divide, where the wind whips up and over the jagged outcroppings of possibility, while the light from distant cities fades behind him, and the atmospheric canopy before him explodes into a visual kaleidoscope and aural cacophony of unrelenting hope. At that very instant, in the rush of that one single moment, he still believes that anything is possible, in spite of the baggage, pain and bitterness that have been his traveling companions. He still believes, perhaps foolishly, that somewhere in that breaking sunlight, somewhere on the road ahead, there might still be healing and redemption waiting patiently for him, ripe for exploding onto his scene. And in that moment, it seems so close, so tantalizingly near, that he can almost smell it like the aroma of Café du Monde wafting down Decatur Street New Orleans, or Hatch green chilies roasting on a September afternoon in Santa Fe.

We pressed on, evenly spaced as we trekked single file, two paces apart. I, our existential engine and engineer, led the way. Uncle Jimmy, the old man, our stabilizer perhaps, was next in line; followed by Tessa, the youthful fuel in our metaphoric mobile machine. Bringing up the rear, with ever-watchful eye, was Teddy Mills, our dark exhaust.

We maintained a steady pace, southwest away from the Studebaker, following what had once been Route 160, hoping to reach the split in the road before dark. There I planned to move into the barren wild of the Painted Desert by morning. We saw only a few fellow travelers, ragged vagabonds, along the way, and like lugubrious zombies, they shuffled their feet to the hypnotic beat of some mesmerizing apathy rhapsody. It seemed as though all hope was gone. Death by doldrums had fallen upon these denizens of desolation, and none made eye contact. They kept their bitter gaze fixed on the dry earth.

All along the harsh hematite horizon, great red spires of rock rose up from the earth all around, jagged edges jutting hundreds of feet into the sky. We courted death there, seeking the intensity of life, pushing ourselves toward peril, four fools in a fearsome, phantasmagoric funhouse. We labored across the mysterious Martian-like landscape, stumbling through thickets of bugleweed and bugloss, mesquite and locoweed, kicking up clouds of red ocher and ruby sulfur, pigments from the Gods, sprinkled down like paprika from the shaker of Zeus all across this other-world.

We reached the intersection where the westward road ended, making a "T" into old Route 89, which ran north and south. This would be our take-off point into the deeper unknown. The earth was revolving us away from the light, and the sky before us was an ominous mesh of bruised purple and angry orange, but we pushed forward leading Bruno through the night. Stopping was foremost on all four of our minds, but none of us wanted to be the one who suggested it. Hours dragged on like a dull knife across our wrists.

I watched my feet, shod in my grandfather's battered boots, trudging wearily along the trail, one determined step at a time, seemingly independent from my brain. I paused to retie the laces, and ran a finger slowly along one boot, tracing a seam from toe to heel. These were the very boots my grandfather wore during World War II in Aachen, Haaren, and Crucifix Hill, in battles that helped break the back of Hitler's horror. He passed them down to me along with his receding hairline, high cholesterol, poor eyesight and penchant for alcohol. All I really wanted were the boots.

After my grandfather's death, my grandmother allowed each member of the family to select a few of his possessions to keep as sentimental souvenirs. My cousin wanted the Japanese saber. My mother wanted his wallet and the pictures he'd carried inside. My grandmother, of course, prized the letters he wrote her during the war. And I took the boots. They were battered and faded in spots to the color of burlap, and some of the hook eyelets were missing, but I didn't care. Though my family thought it foolish, I wanted his boots because they allowed me to walk in his footsteps in a very literal way.

76

My grandfather meant the world to me because he believed in me no matter how badly I thought I'd failed. Where my father berated me, my grandfather encouraged, and I went to him for advice or when I just needed someone to listen. I could talk to him about anything - to my parents, nothing. They didn't see me like he did. They'd never seen me at all.

He often slipped me twenty dollar bills when I was a boy. My parents disapproved of the excessive gifts, so he did it surreptitiously when they were engrossed in some television program or playing canasta with my aunt and uncle. He'd give me a conspiratorial wink and show me just a hint of U.S. Treasury green hidden in his palm. I'd slip over next to him and pocket the twenty. It was the two of us working together to put one over on my parents. He enjoyed spoiling me and twenty dollars was like a million to an eight-year-old in those long-ago days.

It was my grandfather - not my parents – who taught me to drive in his Pontiac Bonneville, fresh off the lot. He purchased the new model every year like clockwork, and the car was more like a small yacht than an automobile. The look on his face was priceless as I, empowered by Leaner's Permit, took that Bonneville too fast down narrow, winding West Virginia back roads. My grandfather tried to keep an even keel to his voice as he suggested I might want to *slow down just a bit*. He gripped the passenger seat and pumped invisible brakes as we wound our way through Glen Morgan, Whitby, Pemberton, Fireco, Jonben and scores of other tiny coal towns that butted up against mine shafts, mountains, and misery.

My grandfather drank. A lot. I never knew why and I never asked him. I simply assumed it was because he enjoyed it. Could there have been some sinister secret or agonizing ache in his soul that drove him back and back to the bottle? Maybe. But to me, he seemed like a happy drinker most of the time; sort of a genial, Otis Campbell type of drunk, although never so disheveled. My grandfather was a neatly-attired, upper-crust alcoholic, always in a crisp white shirt with a modestly designed, dark tie, and an elegant tie clip. I loved those tie clips. When I was small boy, I'd strut around the house with several of them pinned to my shirt, showing off to my mother and grandmother, pretending to be a business man like my grandfather.

One of the best sounds from my childhood was the jangling noise that came from the bedroom when my grandfather emptied his pockets after a long day at work. Tie clip, pocket knife, keys and coins - he always had a mess of loose change - rattled about on the dresser, and I would come running. But that was a long time ago, before my grandfather went to rattle coins on the great dresser in the sky. Now his penknife was in my pocket and his boots were on my feet.

"You okay, Brunky?" Ted asked.

"What?" I answered, looking at him blankly.

"You zoned out, my friend," Ted said, putting a hand on my shoulder. "Are you okay?"

"No," I said flatly, gazing skyward.

"We do not have to do this, you know," Ted offered. "We can go back."

"Ain't no sense standing 'round in the sun," Uncle Jimmy said, interrupting our exchange. "I need some damn water and a sit down."

I nodded toward a culvert and the four of us slipped into slivers of shade in a clutter of rocks and mesquite. We sat in the dirt and drank slowly, careful not to spill a drop of the precious commodity, allowing ourselves two swallows and no more.

"Exactly where are we going?" Tessa asked.

"Judging by the sun, I'd say we're going south," I replied.

"South," Tessa said. "Okay, but where? And why?"

"To see what's out there," I said with a sweep of my hand. "Don't you want to know?"

"I already know what's out there," Ted said. "Rocks, dirt, snakes and heat. My time in the Marines taught me that."

"Do we have enough food and water?" Tessa asked.

"We'll be fine," I answered.

Ted said, "Ever since we were kids, Brunky has gotten us into scrapes that I had to get us out of. Brunky would get a wild hair of an idea, and I would have to follow along to watch his back."

"Does anyone really have any idea where we are?" Tessa persisted.

I squinted against the dying sun and considered the question. "Probably Utah."

"Probably?" Ted said. "Is that the best you can do?"

"Where do you think we are, Uncle Jimmy?" I asked.

"Arizona."

"See," I said, turning back toward Ted. "Arizona."

"You are crazy, Brunky," Ted said, grinning. "You did not used to be, but you are now."

"Only the crazy survive," I said.

The lunar cup was full to the brim, beaming back reflected ancient light to illuminate our desert path. I watched it skirting the horizon, kissing the canyons, dancing with the Kachinas, and was thankful that some things had not changed. The moon remained one huge, bulbous, unblinking eye chewing off chunks of the naked night, peering intensely into our intimates, burning away our dross, exposing our loss, illuminating every dead man's dream and loser's scheme of a hundred billion souls who'd gone before us and a hundred billion more perched on the precipice of possibility.

Then came a howling somewhere from the dark expanse. We stopped abruptly, holding deathly still, listening for long seconds as the eerie, beautiful sound ebbed into oppressive silence. Finally, Uncle Jimmy howled back and we waited for the beast to answer. When it did, he dropped to his knees, mad tears smiling on his ragged cheeks in the moonlight, and howled the howl of old men's dreams of young men's fancies, burned out shells of hopeless faith, and the unquenchable fire of life that kills to eat to live, to kill to eat to live.

Behind me, Ted too began to howl, baying at the moon with his blond locks glowing in the lunar light. Tessa joined him in song and they bent their divergent tones to the tune. All the creatures of the night understood and blended their voices to the cosmic choir. I grasped the paw of Canis Major and the belt of Orion, and, by God, I howled.

On the sixth day post-Studebaker we built a campfire in a gully behind high rocks, huddled near the flames, and ate from our meager rations, too tired for talk. Ted and Tessa tussled together in a single sleeping bag while I entwined my limbs with Emily's ghost and tumbled along the borders of troubled sleep.

I studied her tiny, zippered diary in the moonlight, turning it this way and that, feeling its tattered edges and contours, wondering how something so small could cause a hurt so big, how something so simple could open the door to such mystery.

The wind blew steady and the temperature dipped low. We wrapped our garments around us and pushed forward.

"So, is this what you wanted, Brunky?" Ted asked.

"Yes," I replied, taking a bitterly philosophical stance. "This experience is forcing us to learn about ourselves, to discover what's deep down inside us."

"What about those of us who have already answered that question?" Ted said.

"They can go home, if they choose to," I said.

Ted had been walking abreast of me, stride for stride, and he stopped abruptly, angrily. I turned to face him. He stood erect, his head high, in a military-type pose, but with his hands clasped before him in calm defiance. His blue eyes were stern against his blondish eyelashes, hair and devilish goatee.

"I'm sorry. That was harsh and uncalled for," I said. "I really need a drink." But we had no more strong spirits of which to partake.

Ted looked into my heart and said, "You are forgiven." Then he turned sharply and resumed his pace.

And so we wandered in the desert wilderness for two more weeks, sleeping mostly under the stars. Occasionally we came across an isolated home or village where generous souls gave us food and water. We were ragged tramps and explorers, treading delicately on the eggshells of oblivion.

Twelve vultures watched us warily with black, vacant eyes, but continued on with their business as we approached. Apparently they were having a disagreement regarding the disposition of a horse carcass. Hissing and shrieking, they tore at the equestrian carrion like hillbillies scuffling over knick-knacks at a flea market.

Why twelve vultures? I wondered, tugging on my goat chin. *There were twelve apostles, twelve gates in the Heavenly City in Revelations, twelve months in the year, twelve steps in the AA Recovery program...damn, I wish I had a drink.*

"I don't like the way they're looking at us," Tessa said.

Uncle Jimmy gave her his best rotten-toothed smile. "Darlin', most vultures only eat what's already done its dying." Then he pulled the last draw from his last cigarette and stared banefully at the butt. "Damn it to hell."

"By the by, we shall find you some more smokes, Uncle Jimmy," Ted said.

"*By the by,*" Tessa repeated, grinning, gently mocking her lover.

I suggested to them that cigarettes were the least of our worries.

"Maybe to you," Uncle Jimmy said.

"Don't you ever worry about cancer?" Tessa asked.

"Yeah, right," Uncle Jimmy chuckled. "Won't live long enough t' die from cancer. Hell, I laugh at cancer, thumb my nose at it, flip it the bird."

"Speaking of birds…" A vulture dipped threateningly close to my head, and I threw a stone at it. "I'm not dead yet, you bastard," I called out to the black behemoth.

"Perhaps he knows something you do not," Ted joked.

"Maybe."

Near dusk, we came upon an abandoned building that had once been a small market of some type. It was still standing, but barely. Most of the windows had been broken out, and the door stood open, askew, hanging half off its hinges. The inside had been ransacked and the walls wore a clusterfuck coat of graffiti.

"Reminds me of home," Ted said dryly as we sifted through the clutter.

"Son of a bitch!" Uncle Jimmy shouted. "Look at this!"

He'd found a small rack with a few packs of battered cigarettes buried beneath debris behind the counter. "Lord, it's just like Christmas," Uncle Jimmy said as he stuffed the old Camels and Marlboros into his satchel.

"You can't smoke those," Tessa protested. "God only knows how long they've been there."

"Sweetie, cigarettes age like a fine wine. Hmm, speaking of which, a bottle of Boones Farm would sure hit the spot right about now."

Uncle Jimmy and I were on the same wavelength. That was usually not a good thing.

"Good Lord, Uncle Jimmy," Tessa said with scrunched-up face. "If you're going to wish for something, couldn't you set your sets a little higher than Boones Farm?"

"There ain't no bad alcohol," Uncle Jimmy replied.

It was comforting to sleep indoors, even in a shack, after so long under the open sky, exposed to the elements of nature and danger. If nothing else, it gave the semblance of safety, a temporary haven from the hell we'd been through. We used some aluminum racks and shelving to form make-shift cots to sleep above the floor where roaches, rats, and the unidentified ran through the darkness. It was four walls we could call home for the night.

"Look at them stars," Uncle Jimmy said later, sitting by a window, cleaning his pistol. "Gonna be colder than a well-digger's ass tonight."

"How do you know so much about a well digger's ass?" Ted asked.

Uncle Jimmy pulled the takedown lever and removed the slide and recoil spring on the gun. "That's colder than a witch's tit," he said, wetting the rod with solvent and pushing it through the barrel of the gun. "And I do know plenty about tits."

I stroked my pistol absently as fingers of soft lunar light brushed across my face. I thought I saw, I *wanted* to see the exquisite sparkle of Emily's green eyes somewhere in the shadows. I pictured her exactly as she was the very first time I saw her in that club in Memphis; and though she was gone, and even though her diary had since pushed a veiled heartbreak upon me, I still marveled at her beauty and how much I'd cared for her.

"You're thinking about Emily, aren't you?" It was Tessa intruding on my reverie.

"No," I replied sharply, more harshly than I intended, and then added more softly, "No, just thinking."

"Why is it so hard for you to talk?"

"What do you mean?"

"I mean *really* talk…about what you're feeling and thinking. You keep things bottled up."

"Tessa's right, you know," Ted said.

"I'm talking now," I said in rebuttal.

"No, you don't talk…you dance," Tessa said.

"Okay, I admit it," I said, tugging at my goat chin. "Unless I'm drunk, real conversation is often a challenge for me. I don't know why, but it always has been."

"You *make* it difficult. Talking should be easy…like opening a door."

"Maybe some doors should stay closed, locked even."

"Maybe you should try talking to a therapist."

"Did that once. When I was a teenager, my holier-than-thou aunt Kathryn convinced my father that I needed help, and she set me up for sessions with some Christian psychologist."

"And I bet you didn't really tell him anything, did you?" Tessa said.

"Only what I thought he wanted to hear. I'm smarter than any damn therapist."

"Or so you think. You know the old saying about the blind, right?"

"What? That you can lead him to water but you can't make him drink?"

"Always with the dancing."

"Tessa, the two of you would make quite a pair," Ted said. "Brunky won't talk…and you won't shut up."

Tessa could be like a bulldog.

"God must have given the two of you a very special love," she said, continuing to pressure me for details about Emily.

"Yeah, God," I said flatly. I would not discuss God. Ted and Uncle Jimmy knew that and Tessa should've too.

"The Lord giveth and the Lord taketh away," Uncle Jimmy said, spitting at a lizard, sending his saliva of sarcasm spiraling into the falling darkness.

"I don't know what I believe about God anymore," I said, and closed my tired eyes and rubbed my weary head.

"Faith is really all we have in the end," Tessa said. "I'd rather put mine in a Divine Creator than random chaos. Wouldn't you?"

"Tessa, it doesn't matter what you or I believe," I said sharply, more so than I really intended. "It's all still the same irrational longing and doomed determination with which all humans struggle against the unbreakable bonds of 'how things are' and 'how things forever shall be,' that damnable, immutable destiny into which all have been plunged.

And no matter how desperately, how passionately, we hurl ourselves against the immoveable object, we are no irresistible force. We are merely flesh, bone, and blood – nothing more than the essential components of rich loam filling a green pasture somewhere, someday...ashes and cosmic particles to be carried by currents of wind, sea, and universal karmic waves, stretching from before time to beyond time."

I leaned my head back against the rocks and sighed. "There," I said bitterly, "I talked."

April 1, 1978

We jumped a freight train bound for Albuquerque, rolling into a battered, graffiti-laden box car with a small group of fellow transients. The groan of timbers met the screech of steel rail and wheel with metal couplings slamming and grinding like angry lovers consumed by lust. Inside, frightened families clung together, children huddled beneath mothers' wings. Some men leaned against the walls, pulling hard on cigarettes, their hollow eyes filled with despair and anger, while others were wrapped in rags and California blankets, sprawled about on the grimy floor, sleeping, wheezing, arguing or moaning in delirium. Most of them were victims of the economic downturn that had become a recession which was falling headfirst toward a depression. It was as though we were bounding backwards in our desperately unabated scramble toward a brighter future, and I had the uneasy feeling that chaos and anarchy were eyeing us from behind a grassy knoll.

Uncle Jimmy shared a bottle and cigarettes from his bounty - swapping smokes for swigs - with two hobos who seemed to be about his age, in their early-seventies perhaps. They told dirty stories about dirty towns, guzzling and laughing as Uncle Jimmy rambled on about training across the land in the old days. "When ya jump 'em," he was saying, "ya damn well better jump like the fires of hell are at your backside. I seen a man sliced clean in two, that ain't no shit, neither."

"Yeah...yeah," one of the hobos said, nodding his head slowly. "Awful way to go."

"Sliced him clean in two," Uncle Jimmy slung the words back over his shoulder for the whole car to hear, "Seen it with my own eyes. Damn right."

"Awful way to go," the other hobo repeated and drank to the memory of the unknown railroad victim.

A younger man near the back of the car, seeking a bit of ill-advised entertainment, shouted at Uncle Jimmy. "Why don't you shut the hell up, old man? You don't know shit." The man and his companion laughed.

Truth is, Uncle Jimmy did know shit. Uncle Jimmy was the product of the West Virginia hillbilly mish mash of rugged survivalists, earth-grain types, war veterans, ex-hippies, new age hikers, mountain bikers, coal mine strikers, and an ample portion of typical long-winded, short-sighted, big-bellied, narrow-minded, low-browed, high-cholesteroled, white-bread, middle-class Americans.

Uncle Jimmy's knowledge was that of hard-shell Baptists and snake-handling Holiness hoppers, toil and sweat with no time for regret, and generations of lonely lore and loser's luck hung skewed on a crooked, hillside slant. He'd cut his teeth where Appalachian roads and rivers twisted like drastic pretzels, and houses and automobiles dangled dangerously a thousand feet above crevasses, inches from free-fall. Life lived up a holler on a forty-five degree slant bred a very strange bird, and Uncle Jimmy was one such fowl.

He smoothly slid his revolver from the holster beneath his coat, and pointed it at the man. "No good ever comes from shootin' off your mouth, boy. Didn't your momma ever teach you that?" Then he grinned his ugliest grin and studied a bit, holding the gun steady toward the man's chest.

The young man raised his hands in front of him and wavered with great distress. "Hey, hey, I was just messin' with ya. Come on, buddy, I didn't mean nothin' by it."

Still grinning, Uncle Jimmy put the gun away, "Now that's more like it. A conciliatory attitude does a body good, don't it? But don't get too feisty 'cause I'll be keepin' my eye on you."

I sat on the splintery floor with Ted and Tessa, last night's harsh words long forgotten, and tried to remember when we'd last eaten a hot meal or slept in a real bed. Childhood memories crept out of the dark corners of my mind and bandied about in the light. Lost in spaces between recollections, I tugged thoughtfully on the long strands of my chin hair, the facial tresses I'd grown in high school, back when I'd sought something, as teenagers often do, to differentiate myself from the mindless masses of unremarkable members of our drone-like society.

Ted was the first to use the expression 'goat chin' in reference to my facial hair, and the name stuck. In fact, it became my trademark and signature style - a valuable commodity to any musician. Over the years, I trimmed it, shaped it, and even dyed it occasionally - platinum blonde, crimson red, or brilliant blue - but I never once shaved it off.

So I tugged and drifted through random memories - kissing my first girlfriend over a lunch of seashell macaroni and cheese, throwing up on my favorite teacher in third grade, and chasing a greased pig in seventh grade. Even though my childhood had more than its share of legitimate trauma, it also contained a small measure of lower-middle class stability and innocence for which I sometimes pined. Life may not have truly been simpler then, but I longed for the illusion.

I missed the old house on Phoenix Avenue where I grew up, and the A/C window unit that roared all night like a train rattling the walls of my bedroom. I missed the rough-and-tumble, boyish games of crazy horse, wall ball, and throw-up-and-smear. For generations, life in the civilized world had been composed of such slivers of innocence, relative normalcy, a mass of the mundane interspersed with all too few mad moments of excitement. But now, for the four of us, living had become a blistering blur of danger and passion, fear and hope, like the Painted Desert stretched out before you in the Tucumcari twilight, when it's all you can do to just hold on, grasping handfuls of earth, fingers twined in soil and roots, white knuckles in bluegrass, to keep from spinning out, out into the constellations and exploding into the night like some shooting star of breathless insanity and dangerous wonder.

I wondered if maybe we'd had it wrong all along, if maybe the prosperous ease of Western civilization was simply an aberration, a passing anomaly along the Homo sapiens timeline. Perhaps life was meant to be like this, lived on the unpredictable edge of a vicious razor.

I put an arm around Tessa and Ted and we rode that way for a long while, listening to the locomotive climb, smelling the box car scents of iron, grease and musty wood, strong and good. The clackety-clack was mesmerizing and we swayed with its rhythm, watching the red dirt, cactus and mesquite roll by. A few quaint houses were scattered along the way, with chickens, dogs, and horses skirting the edges of barbed wire fences. There were weather-beaten barns and rusty trucks hauling musty loads along dusty roads. A gaggle of abandoned vehicles stood silently in a field where a great horned billy goat perched on the roof of a junked Volkswagen Beetle. It turned defiantly toward us as we rolled by.

"There's something you don't see every day," I said, "A goat on a bug."

"Hey, he's got your goat chin," Tessa observed, playfully tugging on my blue hair.

A tall man in a long coat stood near the open door and watched the world go by. "She's gone," he said.

"Who's gone?" Tessa asked. "The goat?"

Still staring out at the landscape, the man replied, "America." His voice was forlorn. We gazed with him out at the red dirt, attempting to see what he was missing.

Tessa, ever the inquisitive one, pushed on, "What are you talking about?"

"There is no more America," the man replied, "She's like a lover you fell into bed with for a time. You wooed one another, swore allegiance, and swayed together in the old glory of passion. But all you're left with are soiled sheets and an empty bed."

"Things may not be as you remember them, but America is still alive and well," Tessa said. "Each generation discovers America anew for themselves, on their own terms and in their own way."

"No," the man said, "There's nothing left to discover. The carcass has been picked clean. All this generation can do is lick at the dry bones of what once was. The dream is dead and so are the dreamers."

"You're wrong, dead wrong," Tessa said. "Young Americans still dream. I still dream."

He paid no heed to Tessa. "The dreams of this generation are but shadows cast upon illusions, and the dark and decadent times are coming."

With no warning, the man leaped from the train, his long coat flapping behind him in the wind like angry wings. He hit the ground on a roll, raising a cloud of dust, and sprung to his feet. We watched him run toward the distant mountains until we could see him no more, his figure blending into the landscape, one tiny dot in a massive, crimson kaleidoscope of cacti and rock.

"What a strange person," Ted said.

The box car occupants grew quiet as the day wore into night.   Tessa pressed her head against Ted's chest and yawned. "I'm sleepy," she whispered, barely on this side of dreams.

I stared out at a splash of stars on a coal black canvass, and felt a kinship with a hundred thousand depression-era, dust-bowl-driven transients and bums who once trained their way across the land, seeking a better life wherever the Iron Horse took them. I closed my eyes to the gentle rocking of the locomotive breath, while the warm night air moved through the open car and kissed my hobo cheeks.

Morning broke as it always did, offering up a clean slate and a heaping plate of hope and new possibilities. The sun's warm rays sprinkled tiny rainbows in the dewy grass along the track. With all his grandiose achievements and wicked works, nothing man can ever do can stop the unyielding cycle of Earth and Sun and sky. He might build a tower to the heavens, babbling all the while, or blast himself to freaking kingdom come, but still, the Earth will spin, the sun will shine, and the sky will reach out into eternity.

Ted kissed Tessa's forehead and her dark lashes fluttered as she woke. "Hey, you," he whispered, "Look at the sky."

She stretched toward the light like a cat in feline phototropism. "Mmmm…so beautiful. God gave us another day."

"Not all of us," I whispered.

A woman sobbed softly in the back corner of the car. One of her children, an angel with blonde locks and big brown eyes, had died in her sleep. The little girl had shown no prior signs of disease or disorder, but such are the ways of death. No one knew that better than I did. It struck randomly and unpredictably with no discernible pattern to the fatalities. But everyone's number will come up just as surely as a politician will lie. Some go quietly in their sleep, some go mad with fever, others are cut down by a bullet or car crash or some other definable cause, but we all eventually hit that jagged jackpot according to the plan of God or the Universal Spirit or whatever the hell you wish to call it.

Our box car community lost another life during the night as well – an old man whose clothes were soiled and skin was yellowed. No one seemed to know him, and before anyone could protest, a dark man moved quickly from the shadows, pushed the corpse out of the box car, and crossed himself. The carcass fell from the train like ashes flicked from a cigarette. I scanned the sky for twelve vultures.

Seeing this, the grieving mother clutched the lifeless body of her little girl to her breast and sobbed. She looked toward us, wide-eyed with fear. "Please don't let them take my baby. Please don't. Please."

"No one will touch your child," Ted said firmly, "We promise you that."

Tessa embraced the woman and wept with her. "I'm so sorry," she said, caressing the woman's hair. "What's her name?"

The woman spoke softly, barely audible, choked with grief, "Matilda…her name is Matilda."

"That's such a pretty name."

"She…she," the woman struggled to control her emotions. "She was named after her grandmother." She wiped her eyes and sighed deeply, rocking back and forth, smoothing the girl's golden hair. "They're together now. Isn't that right? She's with her grandma now."

"Yes, and they are in a much better place. I believe that with all my heart."

"I just don't understand why…" The woman shook her head. "Why this happens to my angel?…my sweet baby…my angel."

Tessa and I made eye contact. I moved closer and sang softly, words that I myself had written years before, yet had not fully understood at the time of writing.

Some angels ride the rain,
They come to ease your pain,
Some angels shine and sing,
Then gently spread their wings...and fly...

The woman's bloodshot eyes brimmed with fresh tears, and I held her hand, offering all the comfort I could muster. "I also knew an angel once," I told her.

Soon, the brakes of the Iron Horse took hold and the train ground to a stop, car knocking into car knocking into car, bumpers cracking all down the string of links in the locomotive chain.

Father

April 4, 1978

"What the hell happened to you?" my father said as he opened the door and looked me up and down. "You look like shit."

All three hundred pounds of my father stood in the doorway wearing faded dungarees and a Caterpillar tee-shirt. His hair was silver but his eyebrows were black and thick, and they danced and dueled like a pair of rival ferrets on his forehead as he spoke. He and I were so completely dissimilar in appearance, manner and demeanor, that I often wondered if he was truly my father at all.

"Ted's car broke down," I told him. "We could use a little help here, Dad."

"The car broke down?" He looked around and past me into the driveway. "Well, where the hell is it? Should 'a had it towed here to the house."

Thirty seconds on the front stoop and my father was already irritating the hell out of me. I closed my eyes and took a deep breath.

"We were out in the middle of nowhere and we ran out of money. We've been living on scraps for more than a month."

"Well, what's wrong with the car? Goddamn it, you know I can fix anything on wheels. Let me take a look at it."

"Dad, don't you understand? We couldn't get it here. It broke down out…there…out in the desert somewhere." Frustrated, I gestured in futility, pointing nowhere really.

"The desert? What the hell were you doing out in the desert?" The ferrets appeared angry.

Ted, Tessa, and Uncle Jimmy, not wanting to intrude or seem disrespectful, had remained unusually quiet behind me on the porch during my escalating exchange with my father. Finally, Ted stepped forward to offer assistance, "Mr. Brunk, sir, the engine in my car blew up and we--"

"Teddy...Teddy boy," my father cut him off, shaking his head with disappointment. "You must still be driving the same piece of shit cars that you did when you were seventeen. Do you ever change the oil, Teddy?"

My father was right about Ted and his automobiles. Ted had a lot of cars like the Studebaker when we were teenagers. He was fond of cantankerous, schizophrenic vehicles, those that could run ferociously at times, then suddenly change their minds and play dead.

"Yes, sir, I change the oil."

"What kind you use?"

Ted paused with an irritated hesitation. It was catchy because I felt it too, standing on the porch, being interrogated by an asshole who was also my father. "I think it was Pennzoil," he answered evenly.

"Pennzoil? Jesus Christ! No wonder your goddamn engine blew up." My father was not only an anachronism, but an antagonistic one as well.

No one spoke for a long moment. I looked at Ted and he arched his blond eyebrows at me as if to say, *What now?* Then my father suddenly stepped back and held the door open wide. "Well, what the hell you waitin' on? Are you comin' in or not?"

"Sure, dad."

It must have been six, maybe seven years, since the last time I'd seen it, but my father's mundane house was exactly as I remembered. The same garish picture of faded fruit and forlorn flowers – like those you find in every room of every Motel 6 and Best Western - still hung on the living room wall.   The same drab, tattered furniture still stood upon scuffed legs, firmly set into deep indentations upon the worn carpet that had been in place for decades.   The walls and ceilings were dingy white, smoke-tinted from years of Marlboro mist in the air, and the same wooden pipe holder with tobacco canister still sat upon the same battered coffee table - though, as far as I knew, my father had never smoked a pipe a day in his life.   He was a cigarette man through and through. Finally, and most notably, he still ruled his small kingdom from the same throne he'd had as long as I could remember – a threadbare, gray recliner.   He originally purchased the chair when I was a boy, while mother was still alive, and he moved it with him to Albuquerque after she died, to escape the old home place in West Virginia and the bitter memories it held.

My father led the four of us into the kitchen, and told us to have a seat while he passed out cans of Miller High Life and opened a bag of pork rinds.

"Dad, do you have any real food?"

He looked at me as though I were a block of brie that fell from the moon.

"We've been living on crumbs and scraps for too long. We're hungry."

"Got some lunch meat," he said, bent over, with his head in the fridge.   "Ham, bologna, salami.   There's some Campbell's soups in the pantry."

"That'll work," Uncle Jimmy said.   "We sure appreciate your hospitality."

"I notice you fellas are carrying. Had some trouble or headed for it?"

"Both, I reckon."

My father grunted at that and sucked on his cigarette the way a kid sucks a too-thick milkshake through a straw. Then he turned his attention to Ted. My father liked Ted, always had, but he liked giving him a hard time even more. "Who the hell is this young thing you got on your arm? She a hooker? If she is, she's too good for you."

Tessa giggled and reached over and did the unthinkable - she slid my father's cigarette from his hand and took a long draw. Astonished, he reared back in his seat with a silly grin pasted on his face. I knew what he was going to say before he spoke the words, "I like her."

My father agreed, much more easily than I expected, to let us stay at the house with him for a while. I told him that we just needed a few days to clean ourselves up, get some rest, and put a few good meals in our bellies. He didn't argue. Though he would never admit it, I suppose he'd been lonely for a long time and wasn't about to turn down company, especially visitors as interesting and stimulating as we were. Besides, I was his son...he had to take me in.

That night I stood in the doorway that connected the house with the cluttered garage, drifting through a fog of memories, some pleasant, but most of them uncomfortable. The garage was where my father had always been most comfortable. His countless rows of tools, conspicuously annoying in their perfect arrangement and symmetry, lined and filled the walls. He didn't care much about anything else, but my dad was fanatically persnickety about automobiles and tools. He owned every conceivable type and size of screwdriver, drill, saw, awl, nail, bolt, screw, vise, charger, adaptor, power cord, plumb bob, sander, sandpaper, tape measure and mallet known to man. My father's world was pragmatic, one where he measured things precisely with his tape and then hammered them firmly into place; but he struggled clumsily with things he could not manipulate with his hands – emotions, relationships, death – usually choosing to ignore them completely.

On the far side of the garage, the Green Machine, as it was nick-named, one of the original 1961 Ford Econoline Camper Vans, waited patiently. It seemed to be longing for a revival, anxious for a return to active duty on the open road. Or, at least, that was my hope and an integral part of the plan germinating in the garden of my brain.

The monstrous van had been my father's baby since he first bought it new, constantly cleaning, modifying and fretting over it. The outside was a garish, almost offensive, shade of green, and inside, it was smothered in lime-colored shag carpet. Ironically, for seventeen years, he kept it in perfect running condition, yet rarely drove it. He pored over the mechanical intricacies of the vehicle, pouring his heart into *it*, rather than into *me*, somehow soothing his soul with every twist of the ratchet, tending to it daily as if it were an infant needing constant care.

In my youth, the Green Machine had been my fiercest rival for my father's attention, but now I hoped it would become my comrade, and we would go careening through a cavalcade of cars, swimming in a sea of sedans, ablaze in an array of automobiles, finding our future on Falcon 235/75–15's.

April 20, 1978

A van, a van, my kingdom for a van.

We made up for lost meals and recuperated for a few days that slid slowly into weeks. Dangerously close to wearing out our welcome – with free room, board, and food – we did our best to give my father plenty of space. Ted and Tessa tussled in the bedroom much of the time, their limbs intertwined as in some perverted game of twister. Uncle Jimmy went looking for excitement in downtown Albuquerque, and quickly took a part-time job at the Dirty Rotten, a club on the East side, where he earned enough for smoke and drinks by bussing tables, tending bar, and regaling his customers with tall tales.

Meanwhile, I sought solace in the Sandia Mountains where cacti, sage, and prickly-pear juxtaposed against rust-red rocks and hematite horizons. I wandered daily there, hiking, communing with the spirits, cultivating the dark garden of my soul, and giving thought to the taking of life – one that should have died and one that shouldn't have. Could the former atone for the latter? Would the two cancel each other out and bring me back to zero, balance the scales of my misery? Maybe, but probably not.

I'd learned that in a world where bad was the norm, the only thing that could really surprise me was something good, like love. But even love will eventually leave or disappoint you, just like everything else. Life is cruel and hard like winter in the mountains. Truth is rare and bloody like butchered beef on the chop block. Hope is the foolishness of a blind child tossing coins in a dry fountain. And no matter what spin you put on your life – call it the will of God or put your faith in some unseen hand or leave it at the feet of Jesus – it still all comes out the same in the end. The only viable recourse any of us have is to take action.

My father sat crooked-necked in a straight-back chair, his head tilted far to the left as was his custom. The Marlboro in his right hand surrounded him in a swirling shroud of gray haze, and the Miller in his left left a ring of condensation on the table. Smoke on the water. I sat facing him with a foggy ocean of kitchen table separating us. As a boy, whenever I'd heard the Bible story about Lazarus and the rich man who died, and the great gulf fixed between them in the afterlife, I always thought of my father and me.

Perhaps he was a faithful husband to my mother – I doubted it but could not confirm any indiscretions – but he was a terrible father, a throwback to earlier generations. His parenting skills, and his people skills for that matter, left much to be desired, and he had no interest in improving them. He had guided his household by the old standards. *Children should be seen and not heard. As long as you're under my roof, you'll live by my rules. Shut the hell up and take it like a man. Only pussies cry.* These were but a few of my father's favorite expressions. I was a grown man, but the sting of my father's backhand and a hundred thousand of these callous remarks from my youth were still with me as I faced him that day.

"Look…Dad, I appreciate you letting us stay here," I began.

"Mm huh," he mumbled, beer can to his lips.

"But I guess it's about time we got out of your hair."

"Well, boy, havin' company's like havin' an orgy. It feels pretty good till folks start lining up for the bathroom."

Not quite sure what that meant, I jumped straight to my point. "I need to borrow your van for a while."

The ferrets were perplexed and my father leaned back in his seat as though seeing me from a different angle might help. "You want to take the Green Machine?"

"I really need a vehicle...and I'm asking for your help."

He studied me for a while and drew on his Marlboro like he was trying to suck an answer through the filter. It didn't work.

"I'm asking you respectfully. Please."

"I don't see you for five goddamn years, and then you come rollin' in here and want to take my van without so much as a howdy do."

He shook his silver-haired head and rubbed his whiskers as if trying to get them off his face without a razor. I didn't give a damn. He was my father and *he owed me*. I'd rarely asked him for anything in my life, but I was out of options. There were vultures perched on the windows of my soul.

"It's not like you need the damn thing," I said. "You rarely leave the house, and when you do, you take the pickup. You know as well as I do that the van just sits in the garage most of the time."

"You have any idea how much that vehicle's worth? It's mint condition, boy. I busted my ass on that van for years."

"Yeah, I know."

"Bullshit...bullshit," he muttered to himself, teetering on the verge of resignation. He slowly snuffed his cigarette butt in the ashtray, and took another beer from the fridge, stalling. "Where is it you think you're goin'?"

"I'm not sure yet. Does it really matter?"

"Does it matter?! Of course, it matters."

"Dad, just this one time in my life, couldn't you come through for me? Put me ahead of that vehicle just this once."

Long silence – me staring, him sighing.

"If you put one scratch on that van, so help me, I'm gonna bust your ass. I don't' care how old you are."

My father regularly bought beer by the case, multiple cases at a time, and stored the excess in the fridge in the garage. In the years since he retired, his alcohol consumption had risen in direct proportion to his free time. And so, while the television blathered endlessly and mindlessly in the other room, he and I settled into a temporary truce over a bag of pork rinds and attacked his Miller supply.

I'm long overdue to tie one on. It's been weeks...I deserve to get shit-faced.

We drank liquor with beer chasers – the way real men drink, according to my father – and made typical small talk about the weather, lawn care, what the cousins were up to, which businesses back home had opened up or shut down, who'd been sick and who'd died. And I got shit-faced according to plan. There's just something about mixing hard liquor with rage on the rocks.

Robert Frost once said that he had a lover's quarrel with the world. My life-long lover's quarrel was with alcohol, and it sometimes escalated into a knock-down, drag-out affair. I had similar quarrels with my father, mother, school, and society in general. In retrospect, I suppose my life had been one unending argument.

I never wanted trouble, but it always seemed to find me, whether as a result of my twisted sense of humor, my naiveté, or just plain rotten luck. I spent my entire life trying to do the right thing, striving to never hurt another living soul, yet it seemed as though a myriad of mistakes and a slew of slaughtered casualties followed in my wake. It reminded me of the words of the Apostle Paul: "I do not understand what I do. For what I want to do I do not do, but what I hate I do. What a wretched man I am! Who will rescue me from this body of death?"

So, with the wounds of experience, I was steeped in wisdom born of failure. But I did not crumble. I was trying hard to learn to own my journey, to embrace my pain, and to no longer be an unwilling and unwitting accomplice in the events of my life. I wanted to become the instigator and initiator. One of my own lyrics flowed back to me and I sang drunkenly to my father,

Gonna grab this world, dare to shake it,
Live my life and try to make it
What I want it to be.
I will spread my wings and try
To soar across that great big sky...

"That one 'a yours?" my father asked.

"Yes, it is," I replied sharply, crumpling up an empty pork skin bag and firing it toward the trash can as a sort of exclamation point.

"Hey, where the hell's your guitar? Ain't never seen ya without that thing. 'Course, I don't see ya much, do I?"

"Had to leave it behind, and I don't want to talk about it," I answered.

Astonished, my father asked, "Left it behind? Why the hell'd ya do that?"

"I said I don't want to talk about."

My father shook his head slowly with a sad look of disapproval, and mumbled, "That guitar was the one

110

damn thing in this world that ever made you any money…I just don't understand you…" he trailed off.

Neither of us spoke for a few minutes. We drank our beers and stared at the old tabletop where three decades worth of bottle rings and cigarette burns blended with the wood grain to form forlorn designs.

"What happened to that band you were with?" Dad asked, breaking the silence, tapping the top of his beer can and looking at the ceiling.

"That's over."

"What the hell happened? Last I heard you was doin' pretty well up there in Nashville."

"Our pas de deux was split asunder."

My father's expression was like that of a man staring at the penis of a she-male he'd unknowingly picked up in a bar. "What the hell is that supposed to mean?" he asked, exasperated. "Why can't you ever just speak straight like a man? You been that way since you was a kid, and I never knew what the hell you was talkin' about."

Several ticks of silence beat by as I studied my father's face. "I really wish things could have been different…better between us, Dad."

"And if wishes was fishes, you'd be all scales and gills," he said.

I hung my head and pulled impatiently on my goat chin. My father had sucked the life out of me again and I was suddenly very tired.

"Things just fell apart," I said as I rose and staggered toward the bedroom. "That's the music business."

"Why the hell don't you shave that goddamn hair off your chin?" my father shouted, his words following me down the hallway. "You look like some kinda weird-ass Fu Man Chink."

111

The thin curtains danced softly as the night wind teased them through the open window. I lay on the bed and remembered my Mother, perched uneasily on a wobbly chair, hanging curtains long ago. She'd pricked her finger on one of the brackets, and a single drop of her blood fell from the wound, making a tiny, perfect circle of crimson on the ivory sill. I was only a boy at the time, but I could still remember clearly that stain of hemoglobin hue trickling down from the sill, crawling down the lavender wall, spreading across the hardwood floor, seeping between tongue and groove, soaking my bed in a flood of blood, and painting my entire world an unending red.

I drifted into an unsettling swamp of nightmares where my mother's blood, having long since been pumped from her carotid vein and blended with formaldehyde by some somber embalmer, filled my dreams, swirling alike in the grey matter of my brain and in the dark sewers beneath that distant city.

April 22, 1978

It was strangely cold as Ted and I walked by the Rio Grande, the Great River. Dormant volcanoes eyed us from the pink-sky west as we skipped smooth stones across the quiet water and counted bounces. It was a competition we'd engaged in wherever there was water for as long as we'd known each other. And that was a lot of years.

Brittle branches snapped as we pulled ourselves up a steep hillside through scrub brush and thorns. We stood on a train trestle, feet shoulder-width apart, peering down at the Rio Grande through four-inch gaps between the slick, dark ties.

"I'm ready to get out of Albuquerque," I said.

"Preaching to the choir," Ted replied, pulling his trench coat more tightly around himself. His blondish locks had regained some of their length and wildness in the months since his discharge from the Service. They were now blowing and glowing in the windy moonlight, and his neatly trimmed goatee gave him an air of aristocracy like a dashing prince from some children's fairy tale.

"Where do you want to go next?" Ted asked.

I shook my head slowly. "We got nowhere to go...and everywhere to go. Weird, isn't it?"

A low rumble crawled down the track toward us from the mesa and the trestle began to tremble. A train sliced through the darkness, closing fast, and we crouched between the timbers along the side rails of the bridge.

The steel blue BNSF engine roared by so close we could smell its locomotive breath, and we did the madman scream with tears of fear and joy.

As the train faded away, we sat between the timbers with our legs dangling over the side of the trestle, just as we had when we were boys.

Ted said, "Hey, remember the night that state trooper ran us off that CSX bridge?"

"Oh, yeah, I remember," I laughed. "He couldn't believe we had the gall to build a fire in the center of a train trestle."

"The look on his face was priceless," Ted said, laughing as he shifted into his best southern-drawl-state-trooper impersonation. "You boys know you're smack dab in the middle of a train track, don't ya? You're trespassin' on official property of the CSX railroad. I'm gonna give you two minutes to extinguish that fire and vacate these particular premises."

"You sound exactly like him," I said, leaning over the bridge, laughing.

"Vacate these particular premises," Ted repeated with an even more exaggerated emphasis on the southern accent, practically drooling on the drawl.

"How about the time," I said, "that you begged me to shoot you in the foot so that you could get out of the Marines?"

"I did *not* beg. Besides, what are best friends for?"

"I never understood why you didn't just shoot *yourself* in the foot."

"Did you ever try to shoot yourself? Unless you intend to kill yourself, you will find it's not so easy, my friend."

Night was falling silent. I threw a red rock that kerplunked sullenly in the black river below us. Neither

114

of us said a word for a long time. Finally Ted spoke softly, "I wish I could have really gotten to know Emily."

"Me too," I said. "She was just so…different, melancholy, glorious…hard to find the right word. She was beautiful inside and out…and yet, obviously, there was a lot of darkness and sorrow there too." I paused and then added, "And, apparently, secret deceptions, as well."

Ted studied me, commiserating, his blue eyes wet with compassion. "What do you mean…deceptions?"

I ignored the question, and continued, "Maybe one of my favorite memories of Emily is the best way to describe her. Once, right in the middle of a terrible thunderstorm, she ran outside and danced in the downpour. Wicked lightning was flashing all around – it even blew up the transformer beside our apartment – but Emily just kept on dancing in the rain until I came out and joined her."

"She was an incredibly complicated woman, wasn't she?" Ted observed.

"That's for sure. She could be so bold and engaging at times, and yet, was so full of neuroses, phobias and demons. She was, and still remains, an enigma to me. I miss her so much, but sometimes I'm not sure what to feel about her anymore. I guess we all do things we regret…"

"I don't understand. What regrets?"

I shook my head. "Nothing…forget it."

Ted and I pondered the memory of Emily storm-dancing while a speechless sky of silent stars stared down our souls, and ghost-eye headlights led phantom automobiles along yellow lines toward darkened destinations.

Uncle Jimmy threw me a left hook that I leaned into.

"Listen, Brunky, I don't know no other way to break it to ya 'cept to say it straight out. I'm stayin' here in Albuquerque for a while."

Surprised, I stared at the old man. "You're kidding."

"Nope. Gave it some hard thought and decided I've done enough traipsin' round the country chasin' wild-ass schemes. I was lookin' for a change, and I found it right here. Met me a Navajo woman down at the club and we done sparked together real good. God Almighty, she could raise the pecker on a dead man. I'm movin' in with that girl. Ain't never loved an Indian before."

"Well, I guess you have to do what your heart tells you to."

"Or your dick," he said, laughing. Then he leaned in close to me, put a hand on my shoulder, and spoke as gently as I'd ever heard him speak. "Now, you listen to me, Brunky, I know what you're goin' through. I been on this earth a long time, and suffered more than my share of heartache. Buried a lot of family and friends and it ain't never easy. But I'm tellin' ya for your own good, Brunky, you got to move on. Emily's gone and it's a shame, a *damn* shame. But she's gone."

"Gone," I whispered.

"But you're still here. Listen to what Teddy boy's been tellin' ya. It don't do one damn bit of good for the livin' t' fret about them that's gone."

116

"I don't need anyone to tell me how to grieve."

"C'mon, Brunky, why not stay a while here with your old man? You could git yourself a job--"

"Stay here longer with my father? I don't think so."

"All you're gonna' do is keep the whole mess slung around your neck like a damn albatross. And it's gonna bring ya down, Brunky."

"One man's albatross is another man's phoenix," I said.

"Ah, bullshit. You don't listen to a damn thing." Uncle Jimmy waved his hand dismissively, and stood up. "And I guess you're gonna drag Teddy around the countryside with ya too?"

"Ted can make up his own mind. If he wants to come with me, he can."

"Don't play cutesy with me. You know damn well that boy's gonna back you up all the way."

He was right and I knew it. Ted had stayed by my side, and I by his, through waters too thick to drink and too thin to plow. There is a friend that sticks closer than a brother, and Ted was that.

Suddenly, he and Tessa entered the room and the conversation. "Speak of the devil," I said, managing a weak smile. "It's his right hand man."

"And...his mistress," Tessa said with a mischievous smile and an exaggerated, girlish curtsy. She then morphed smoothly from that position into her cat and crane martial arts stances. "So when are we leaving?" she asked.

"Maybe tomorrow, maybe the next day."

"And where are we going, fearless leader?"

"Don't know yet. Anywhere but here."

"Okay. So we're just gonna jump in that big, green van and drive?" Tessa asked.

"Exactly."

117

I dreamed, reels spinning once more on my pons projector. A vicious vulture gripped me in its talons, spread its powerful wings, and carried me high above the Painted Desert. Its claws sliced into me, bringing a flow of bright blood that fell toward the dark earth where stony, scarlet spires shot skyward from the red dirt, and menacing monoliths stood like massive haystacks of horror.

Far below, Emily and my mother stood silently with arms raised heavenward, reaching for me, waiting for me in the still point of my turning world. The great bird released me and I plummeted downward, dream-screaming with my blood streaming, gleaming in the moonlight beaming. The frigid wind roared in my ears and bit my skin with tiny teeth as I spiraled into the arms of my captors.

Green Machine

Ted, Tessa, and I said our goodbyes, sparse and brief, to Uncle Jimmy and my father in the cold, pre-dawn Albuquerque air. I put the keys in the ignition of our future and turned them, and the Green Machine roared to life. I backed my father's precious van out of his garage and whispered to Ted and Tessa, "Enough with the sitting still. Let's see what we can find out there this time." But I don't think they heard me. We weren't even out of my father's driveway, and the two of them were already squirming, giggling and making out in the back.

The sky was a crisp black canvass, and the stars were dancing on their tiptoes one final hurrah before the sun put them to bed for the day. The traffic lights were flashing yellow, and the streets were quiet as we pulled out at 5:19 am. And though there was dark portent on my distant personal horizon, we were giddy as third-graders, high as kite strings in leap year. Of all life's ecstasies, nothing compares with *going*.

I believed our cause to be noble, and we were caught up in the thrill of setting out on the road again with a mysterious mission in mind. We were tracing the template that was uniquely American – the merging of minds, the convergence of cultures, and the unquenchable quest for zest with the worst unending thirst to first burst forth upon this world with an explosion of energy, heeding the ancient call of Columbus and Magellan, leaving a flat world behind for one whose curvature dipped precariously into the shadows.

In my early twenties, before the band began to have some success, I'd lived in my share of dead ends, flipping burgers and delivering pizzas to make a buck. I'd even done a short time on the assembly line of the corporate ladder, crunching numbers and churning out pie charts and power-point demonstrations. So, as we veered once more toward new adventures, I felt myself poised on the precipice of possibility, crossing my Great Divide, and doing it for all those cubicle-constrained comrades, for all those battering on or battered by mouse and keyboard, email and IM, phone and headset, video-conferencing and sales calls. We were doing it for all the victims of laborious, tedious, repetitious, assembly-line processing, manual labor, with broken back and broken spirit, and bored beyond measure by the vast, endless, meaningless, pointless exercise in futility known as Modern American Life.

We idled at the intersection of interstates 40 and 25. North, east, south, west – each one offered us a unique and pristine path filled with infinite possibilities. The choice was ours and our future rested on a whim.

"Which direction, mister man?" Tessa asked.

I turned sharply toward her.

"What's wrong?" she asked, her eyes wide.

"Emily used to call me 'mister man.' It was a silly pet name she had for me."

"I'm, I'm sorry," Tessa stammered. "I didn't know."

"It's okay. You couldn't have known. It just caught me off guard, that's all. I've never heard anyone but her use that expression. I haven't heard it since…"

I got out of the van and stood in the road, tugging intently on my goat chin. Ted and Tessa exchanged nervous glances, watching me. The sky was beginning to brighten on the eastern horizon, and I raised my hands heavenward and let the stiff wind move me. A passing motorist swerved to miss me, horn blaring, but I paid no mind.

Climbing back into the van, I said, "With so much darkness in my soul, it only seems logical we should head toward the light."

And so we went east on 40.

"A hunch is the hinge on which the door of destiny swings," Ted said as we rushed to meet the sun.

We rolled through terrain where aliens in UFO's once plunged to their deaths, where centuries of horrors were heaped upon Native Americans, and where atomic bomb experimentations and detonations were conducted, as man sought ever more ways to inflict misery upon man. The land held so many varied vibrations and queer quarks of energy, and we perambulated with no parameters, flying by the seat of our pants over terrain so strangely beautiful.

At Santa Rosa we left the interstate and drove to Fort Sumner where Kit Carson and the United States government once enslaved thousands of Navajos and Apaches simply for the crime of not being white. The little town had become a tourist trap where masses of merchants cheerfully sold their wares atop mounds of massacre and misery. Tessa, ever the explorer, took it all in stride and insisted we see the grave of Billy the Kid, and the house where Pat Garrett shot him down. I popped the appropriate cassette into the player, and Bob Dylan's haunting voice and music filled the Green Machine with the gunslinger's lonesome story.

Somewhere in the high plains of north Texas, we gathered round our cooler at dusk, and feasted on a bounty of cold beer and bologna sandwiches – thick deli slices on fresh white bread.

"Did you know," Tessa said, mouth full of sandwich, mustard on her chin, "That your thymus gland disappears after puberty?" Tessa was the queen of trivia, and she thoroughly enjoyed dropping obscure tidbits of random information into ongoing conversations or awkward silences.

"Then I suppose Brunky still has his," Ted said.

"Damn straight," I countered. "And my thymus is twice as big as yours."

"Be serious," Tessa said.

"I was not even aware that I had a thymus gland," Ted said. "Where does it go when it disappears?"

"I hear it leaves a note saying it's going out for a pack of cigarettes, but it never comes back," I said.

"Or perhaps…" Ted said in his creepiest, exaggerated Vincent Price voice, "It crawls up your esophagus and out your mouth while you're sleeping."

Tessa tore off a piece of her bread, wadded it up in a ball, and hit Ted in the forehead with it.

"Then it finds seven other thymus glands more evil than itself," Ted continued, undeterred, quoting the words of Jesus in the Gospel according to Mark, "And proclaims 'We are Legion for we are many', and they return to live inside you, and the state of that man is worse than the first!"

"You are an intellectually challenged donkey," Tessa said, kissing him, blending her mustard with his. "But you're *my* donkey, and a girl can only work with what she's got."

Later, for a long while, we lay on our backs and stared at the stars.

"Listen to the earth," Ted said. "You can almost hear it spinning."

"This reminds me of a certain beautiful night outside Pittsburgh," I said. "Emily and I held hands and watched the stars, just like this. Then we made love on the hood of a truck."

"Well, don't get your hopes up," Ted laughed. "That's not happening tonight."

"The hood of a truck? Sounds uncomfortable," Tessa added.

We built a fire and I reclined close to the popping, cracking wood, and read Emily's diary once again by the light of the flames. Her words were like burning embers in my soul. Ted and Tessa were deep in slumber, her body wrapped around his, but my sleep was like a pencil behind my ear that I could not find. So, sitting quietly between locoweeds and bugloss, I waited for the sunrise and toasted it with a beer when it arrived.

Reluctantly, Ted, Tessa, and I left our little spot on the prairie and wandered, wondering if what world we'd witnessed was the one we'd wished. We followed roads that morphed into trails that dead-ended at ramshackle houses hedged by twisted posts and rusty barbed wire. We passed fields of evil trees, black and charred, with jagged branches like brittle fingers reaching upward. We drove herky-jerky through Turkey, Texas, and blew the horn in honor of Bob Willis. We edged through Estelline where a sign on the south side read "Population 194," and a similar sign on the north end proclaimed "Population 168."

"Heads will surely roll in county government when they notice that glaring mistake," Ted observed.

"Maybe they're droppin' like flies around here," I laughed.

Two days more, three days even, we traveled in fits and starts, circles and tangents. It's a long road when you've got nowhere to go. We saw a red-nosed clown in full clown regalia, driving a battered '72 Nissan pickup with two ragged Mexicans stern-faced in the back. The sky was Dodger blue as we passed them on the yellow-lined blacktop and waved. The Mexicans returned our greeting, but the clown kept his funny hands at ten and two.

Somewhere on Oklahoma Route 152, between Cloud Chief and Dill City, we came upon a bright blue sofa on the side of the road, inches from the pavement. A man sat cross-legged on the couch, seemingly oblivious to the world around him.

We stopped. Tessa introduced herself and plopped down beside him on the roadside sofa.

He was a very old black man with orange hair and a long beard – heavy on the salt, light on the pepper – that reached to the third button on his neatly pressed white shirt. His pants were khakis and his shoes were penny loafers with nickels in the slots. He carried an impressive mesquite cane with an intricately carved dragon's head topper. His name was Seventy-Six.

"That's an unusual name," Tessa giggled. She was unbearably cute when she laughed, and she laughed often. She pulled a bluestem stalk from the roadside weeds and spun it between her fingers absently. "Are you thirsty? We have a cooler full of cold drinks."

"I crave Dr. Pepper," he said. "Do you have any?"

"We don't go anywhere without it. Ted, will you get Seventy-Six a Dr. Pepper? Get one for me too, please."

Ted stroked his goatee, smiled like a sheepish cat, his azure eyes gleaming, and did as she asked. He brought me a beer.

"That's my boyfriend, Ted W. Mills," Tessa said, pointing. "And that's Brunky, our fearless leader."

I shook his hand and he studied me. "Leader? That implies some sort of mission."

"We are on an adventure," I replied.

"Is your name truly Seventy-Six?" Ted asked.

"For now." He savored the Dr. Pepper like a blind man savors Tchaikovsky's Fifth Symphony, "But I change it about once a year."

"Why are you sitting out here?" I asked.

"I was waiting for you."

"Right," I said with a sliver of sarcasm.

"Well, you came, didn't you?"

128

He had me there.

"You should ride with us." Tessa said excitedly.

"Where are you going?"

"We don't know," I said.

"That's *exactly* where *I'm* headed," Seventy-Six said.

"But what about your couch? We don't have room–" I said, hoping to discourage him. It wasn't that I didn't like the old man – I did – but rather, I typically didn't embrace people as readily as Tessa did.

"Don't worry about the couch; possessions are highly over-rated," he replied, cutting me off. "Things are what they are, you know, and nothing more than we make them."

Somewhere in Arkansas, a storm took hold of the sky and hurled rain against the Green Machine as if to stop it in its tracks, and, having no success, threw hail at it as well. It was one of many foreboding meteorological discontents, and we pushed against it, accompanied by an army of eighteen-wheelers. Lost and lonely little towns shivered in the cold wind, nearly swallowed up by the angry, low-riding clouds.

"Devil's fighting with his wife," Tessa shouted as the thunder cracked like the iron skillet of God on the stone heads of Mount Rushmore.

There were grey skies, as well, rolling into my grey matter, an overcast dream taking over my brain, hurling cosmic drops of sadness from synapse to synapse. I stared through the windshield into the future, the van doing sixty-five, and my mind a thousand miles per hour. Memories scraped through my mind like a Corvette over speed bumps, while, in the back, Tessa, Ted and Seventy-Six shared shots, smokes, and stories.

"We have too long been an Orwellian society slobbering at the fetid feet of the God of Technology, a hedonistic, imperialistic, plastic, soul-less empire of which the Mesopotamians, Byzantines, and Hittites could have only dreamed. This nation has been awash in ceremonial cavalcades of corruption, while the average citizen stumbles in the shackles of servitude and flounders in the frying pan of life," Seventy-Six said.

We chewed on that for a while and watched the wipers whip back and forth. I swerved to miss the remnants of a Goodyear that had obviously had a bad day.

"Arkansas must have more billboards with scripture than any other state in the Union," I observed. "I guess the Razorbacks strap their Bible Belts on tightly."

"Mr. Ted, Mr. Ted," Seventy-Six said, an arm draped around Tessa's shoulders, "You are a very fortunate young man. Do you realize what you have in this magnificent young vixen? You are the luckiest of men!"

"Oh, do go on now," Tessa said, doing her very best southern belle impersonation. "I do declare, you're giving me the vapors."

"I tell you this, Mr. Ted...be glad that I am not a younger man, for I would surely dazzle Miss Tessie with my wily charms, and sweep her gloriously off her delicious feet and directly into my arms." He winked at Tessa and she kissed him adoringly on the cheek.

We rolled on, biting off chunks of the Ozark State, as I guided the Green Machine over brown earth.

"I suggest we set forth for Shreveport and visit my wife," Seventy-Six said. He felt completely comfortable in making ex cathedra pronouncements at the drop of a hat, or at the drop of nothing at all.

"You're married?" Tessa said. "Good thing you told us...I was just about to make my move on you."

"I haven't seen her in three years," Seventy-Six said.

"Why not?"

"I've been quite busy."

"I foresee a tense reunion," Ted said.

We pointed the Green Machine toward the Gulf, and dug into the thick Louisiana air along Route 71. Four hours later, twilight tipped the sky toward black as the van lumbered up a narrow trail where thick stands of sweet gum, magnolias, and bitternut hickories scraped their arms against the sides and top of the van. The air smelled like alligator breath. Houses were few and far between, and most were rat-trap structures with clapboard siding. Rusted automobiles rested up on cinderblocks, hedged about by tall grass and discarded household appliances. Gruesome figures staggered along in the darkness like apocalyptic foreshadowers, paying no heed to the oncoming vehicle. Our headlights illuminated a ghostly scene inhabited by men, women, children, dogs and goats.

"Are you sure we're on the right road?" I asked.

"Patience, my young friend," Seventy-Six replied.

"This looks like humanity's distant past," Ted said.

"And our rapidly approaching future," I added.

Dark Eyes was standing, hands on hips, at the north corner of her southern-sized, wraparound porch as we rattled up to the house. She was dark-skinned and tall, wearing a bright yellow, button-up shirt, tight jeans and cowboy boots. Her hair was long and silver, adorned with multi-colored beads and small feathers. Her smile was big as all the world and she glowed in the moonlight.

"I could feel you coming!" she shouted, coming down from the porch.

"Hello, squaw," Seventy-Six said as they embraced warmly. He caressed her hair and she tugged tenderly on his long beard.

"You always come back," she said.

"And you're always waiting for me."

They kissed for an uncomfortably long time. He dipped her, and in turn, she dipped him. Finally, they turned their attention to the three of us. "Well, Clancy, I see you've brought some interesting company down to the swamp."

"Clancy?" Tessa and I said simultaneously, looking askance at Seventy-Six. He certainly didn't look like a Clancy to me.

Inside the house, Dark Eyes introduced us to her friend Karl. "That's Karl with a K," he informed us. "I'm a hog hunter."

"A hog hunter?" Tessa asked, her cute face scrunched up with a puzzled look.

"Damn straight," Karl responded simply, with no additional information, as if an explanation for such a line of work could not possibly be necessary.

Karl was tall and lanky, as white as a white boy could be. He was shirtless with long, brown hair cut in a perfect mullet, and he must have been at least thirty years younger than Dark Eyes.

"I'm Brunky with a B," I said, extending my hand. "Pleasure to meet you."

"Bitchin' hair," Karl said, pointing to my chin. "Rock n' roll." Then he gulped from his can of Busch beer and slid next to me. "You ever kill a hog with a bow?"

I pondered the question, giving the impression that perhaps I had at some point killed a hog with a bow and arrow, but had forgotten exactly when it occurred.

"Karl's been staying with me for a few months," Dark Eyes said, jumping into the conversational lull. "I feed him and keep a roof over his head, and in return, he helps me around the farm and keeps me company in the bedroom. A woman has needs, you know."

"Damn straight," Karl said.

I glanced at Seventy-Six but he showed no sign of surprise or irritation at his wife's admission.

Tessa whispered to Ted, "Considering his looks and personality, Karl must be *really* good in the bedroom."

That evening we feasted fabulously on crawdad gumbo, red beans and rice, fried green tomatoes, boiled potatoes, cornbread, sweet tea and moonshine. After dinner we migrated into the sitting room and settled upon furniture straight from the set of *Gone with the Wind* – a mauve divan, a lavender canapé, and a large plush sofa. We drank and smoked and told countless stories, regaling the past and condemning the future; then reconsidering, we regaled the future and condemned the past.

Thoroughly liquorated, Seventy-Six, our loquacious, garrulous sesquipedalian began to sermonize like a Pentecostal in the Spirit, rhythmically tapping his exquisite cane on the hardwood floor as he paced back and forth, back and forth.

"In spite of all our mental meanderings," he said, "our rambunctious escapades, accumulation of possessions, philosophical philandering, loves and losses, foolhardy

134

schemes, endless hopes, and hopeless dreams, men are still like the ants. We march in dutiful lines, droning our way toward the queen, with the sum total of a million haunting, yearning years of need, and a billion undulating past-life regressions and futureless life-force progressions screaming into this one single NOW. There is nothing else, my friends. *Nothing* else." He punctuated the air dramatically with his cane as he reached his didactic climax, arm jerking to and fro like some mad maestro.

Dark Eyes watched him intently, yet he did not look her way. "Do you no longer believe in heaven or a hereafter?" she queried.

"Heaven," Seventy-Six said, spitting the word out. "Heaven is Hell's reflection in Lake Pontchartrain."

"Heaven?" he repeated, picking up an old, grade school class picture from a shelf, holding it up for us to see. "Look upon these children. Heaven is in these hopeful faces facing a hopeless future, with undreamed dreams and unseen visions, so full of promise, so foolishly naïve, not knowing that fate is the fulcrum on which the lever of life shall ever turn." And then he quoted the words of the poet Michael Crisp,

> *March us out, one by one,*
> *March us out into the morning sun,*
> *Where fields of wheat and goldenrod,*
> *Stretch their arms toward the hand of God,*
> *Perambulators is all we are,*
> *Traversing sand and sea and star.*

For a moment, the only sound in the room was Karl drawing deeply on his unfiltered Camel.

"Heaven? Streets of gold and pearly gates?" Seventy-Six continued, dripping with sarcasm. "Yes, and I am

135

certain there are also three-legged moon men raising a ruckus in the Sea of Tranquility."

He stopped and glared into Dark Eyes' dark-eyed stare, opprobrious sparks between them, and perhaps another flavor of sparks as well. A small lamp cast its sixty-watt glow in a far corner, some candles flickered yellow, and cigarette tips glowed orange-red. It was a tall moment in a serious room.

"And what would you know...of tranquility?" Dark Eyes whispered.

May 12, 1978

I slept in a tiny peach room with paint that was peeling from the heavy, humid air. I lay in what must have once been a child's bed for it was too short for me to stretch fully out. Behind the headboard and below the shadowed dormer peak was a window, and I stared out at pinpoint spots of light that sparkled with pen-drop silence as they poked through the blackened canvass of the Cajun night. With my arms across my chest in the position of deathly repose, I thought of my mother and Emily.

Just before dawn, I slipped downstairs and took a beer from the fridge just like my father would have done. No one else was stirring, so I stepped quietly onto the front porch. Seventy-Six and Dark Eyes were wrapped in a blanket together on an old metal glider, fast asleep. Karl, however, was nowhere to be found. I smiled, slightly amused, but not terribly surprised. I supposed anything was possible with Cajuns.

I sat silently for a long while on the top step of the front porch, sipping the perfect beer on the perfect morning. Ants ran missions around my feet, carrying tiny bundles, only God knew why and where, and egrets chattered, speaking to each other and perhaps to me. "Yes, my friends, it's a new day," I whispered, raising my bottle to them. "You have your missions – I have mine."

Two hours later, everyone was stirring and the house was filled with the wafting, blending aromas of coffee, bacon, bourbon, magnolias, and even cow pies from an adjacent pasture. Tessa was holding her Flying Insect

Pose in the living room as she ran through her morning routine of advanced Yoga and Tae Kwon Do progressions. In the kitchen, Ted was experimenting with scrambled eggs, feta cheese, and Louisiana hot sauce, and singing, as he so often did, "Bridge Over Troubled Water."

"Perm that hair," I said, "And you'd be a dead ringer for Art Garfunkel."

We partied for days in the Shreveport swamp. The house brimmed with dozens of people named Billeaudeau, Cheramie, Champagne, and Meriepoiu who descended on the farm with gumbo, bread pudding, liquor, potato salad, guitars, banjos, fiddles, buckets of shrimp, and kegs of beer. They drank hard and played loudly with Zydeco zealots and Cajun commandos clashing in musical combat as the crowd danced through the house, onto the porch, and out into the tall grass. Each afternoon, after an appropriate amount of alcohol consumption, we played a variation of American football called drunken football, which, fortunately, resulted in nothing more than minor bruises and lacerations.

In the evening, we built a bonfire in a clearing not far from the Red River, near a stand of Water Oaks and Southern Magnolia, and shared stories, telling tales both tall and true. In the dark shadows of the dancing fire, hemmed in by those towering sentinels, Ted took off his boots and gave a moving recitation, from memory, of the full text of Edgar Allan Poe's "The Raven." Ted's entrancing voice and flair for the dramatic could have easily convinced a stranger that he'd studied Shakespeare at Eton.

With his final "Nevermore," he weaved and wobbled on uncertain legs, downed the last of his drink, lowered himself gingerly into the grass, and fell immediately asleep. Eschewing the small bed in the peach bedroom, I lay at his side that night and we snored together, brothers beneath a swampy moon and Cajun constellations.

May 16, 1978

I woke, blinking into a purple-gray sunrise canvas with dew settled on my face, and dandelions and white clover whispering in my ear. I staggered through the brush and peed yellow down by the Red River, naked to the world and not ashamed. Bare feet to the soil, bare soul to the burdens I'd borne, I experienced an extemporaneous epiphany – I was seeing things more clearly, my goal coming into focus.

I'd wasted the first half of my life on a youthful mission to impose order on chaos, wavering on the winds of uncertainty, like balancing English peas on a butter knife while riding the Cyclone at Coney Island. I was determined to break the cycle, resolved to become the little gun with a big bang, a projectile with a purpose.

I shook Ted gently. "Rise and shine, my friend. Surely you're not going to sleep this entire day away."

The word "hangover" hung up somewhere between Ted's larynx and palate as he vomited in the clover. When he finished, he leaned back on his elbows in the grass and calmly grinned his devilish grin. "Must have been something I ate."

The front screen door whined as Tessa came out and joined us. "What're you dashing drunkards up to this lovely morning? Did you sleep well?"

"I slept barely a wink," I said.

"How about you, Teddy? Are you ready to face the day?" Tessa leaped upon Ted and they rolled in the grass, laughing and loving.

141

"Maybe I'll just kick your ass while I'm down here," Tessa said playfully.

"Even in my weakened state, you have no chance," Ted said.

"Oh, yeah?" Tessa shouted as she entangled her fingers in his golden locks and twisted hard.

"You fight like a girl," Ted yelped.

"Sweetheart," she said with an evil grin. "I could have you begging for mercy using any number of methods."

"I definitely do *not* doubt that," I observed from the fringes of the fray. "Hey, the sun's up above the horizon and we haven't had any vodka." I retrieved a bottle from the Green Machine and took a long swig. "Who's with me?"

"Lord, no," Ted said. "I need food, not drink. Some of Dark Eyes' biscuits and gravy would hit the spot."

As if on cue, the screen door whined again and Dark Eyes stepped out to call us inside. "Breakfast is on the table. Come get it while it's hot. It'll do you good."

We went inside for sausage, gravy, cheese biscuits, fresh tomatoes, and coffee black. After three days of partying, the last of the neighbors and relatives had finally gone home, and the house was strangely quiet as the five of us – Ted, Tessa, Seventy-Six, Dark Eyes, and I – sat around the dining table.

"What happened to Karl?" Tessa was bold enough and inquisitive enough to finally ask.

Surprised, Ted and I looked up at her sharply.

"Tessa," Ted said softly with a hint of reproach.

"What?" she replied, "Hey, I want to know. You can't know if you don't ask."

For several minutes, Dark Eyes and Seventy-Six continued eating breakfast, seemingly unfazed by the question hanging in the air. Finally, with a mouth full of cheese biscuit, Seventy-Six said, "She's right. One must ask if one wishes to know."

Forks poised in mid-air between bites, we waited for the answer.

"The boy went hog hunting," Seventy-Six said, smiling as wide as a semi full of fat back. "I told him we'd spotted that monster hog up near Blind Hole."

"Monster hog?" Tessa said.

"There is a monster hog that lives in the swamp," Dark Eyes explained.

"That's what they say," Seventy-Six said with a shrug of his shoulders. "It's supposed to be a vicious razorback the size of a Volvo."

"Two-door or four-door?" Ted asked.

"Karl's mission in life is to kill that hog," Dark Eyes said. "And so off he went."

"Off he went," Seventy-Six said with a grin.

"Nothing more inspiring than a man with a dream," I said.

Shreveport shrank in the rear view mirror as the radio blasted the extended version of "Radar Love," the epitome of Dutch rock and roll. I drummed along on the steering wheel, and pushed the Green Machine to ninety miles per hour due west across Interstate 20, barreling back into Texas.

For a while, Ted and Tessa tussled in the back, twin tunes tied by one towering true love. I stole secret glances at them in the rear view mirror as they kissed passionately, her hands in his hair, her tongue in his mouth, his hands fondling her breasts. I was happy for them. *I'm happy for them*, I reminded myself. Though, truly, I was jealous that they had each other, while I had no one. I conjugated the complex entries on my personal ledger, tumbling down a literary landfill of mixed metaphors, anguished allegories, and hopeless hyperboles. I was becoming badly bipolar with no equator, no center line to reign me in. I stroked my goat chin absently and sang softly to myself:

Orbits come and orbits go
But you're the only planet I know
The golden orb has broken through
Copernicus revolving you, uh huh
You and I are jagged edges,
Piece by piece we come,
Far apart and far so near,
Dreaming, dreaming in the sun...

Ted and Tessa counted cows and horses, doubled them at the churches, buried them at the cemeteries. They played punch buggy, board games, War and Blackjack, while I considered the miles of unyielding pavement that rolled beneath us, a scant eighteen inches from our feet, separated from us only by thin layers of metal and carpet.

I thought about how smoothly the Green Machine operated, steady on the course no matter the obstacles, always faithful and dependable. It occurred to me that, in a very real sense, machines were better than people, and that perhaps that was why my father had poured himself into this vehicle, because no matter what went wrong, it was still a machine and *it could be fixed*. You simply ordered new parts, you disassembled and reassembled, you added fluids, you tuned it up, and it ran like new. People were not so easy to repair, sometimes even impossible, and eventually they left you forever. *I guess the bastard was smarter than I ever gave him credit for*.

I stared through the bug-splattered windshield, musing, and had the feeling that someone far away was calling my name.

"Brunky, Brunky…I'm trying to tell you something." It was Tessa, attempting to break the spell under which I'd fallen.

"What?" I said, glancing at her in the rearview mirror. "Were you talking to me?"

"Brunky, I'm really worried about you. You seem so withdrawn much of the time and your temper's short. Something is eating at you and you've changed."

"We all change," I said dismissively.

"I am afraid I must agree with Tessa," Ted said.

"I have a lot on my mind," I replied. "Demons are nipping at my heels."

"Maybe you should slow down, think things through, and talk to the people that care about you."

I chewed on beef jerky, sipped a little vodka, and ignored them for a while. But I should have paid heed.

Why is it so hard to bring ourselves to do the things we know we should?

My mood was quickly turning as black as the Slab Fork coal dust that once burrowed into every pore of my great-grandfather's skin, and settled an inch deep in his tin lunch bucket. I was riding recklessly toward the city limits of Unhingedville.

May 24, 1978

We drifted north for a few days, and somewhere near Flagstaff, Arizona, Ted, Tessa and I floundered in a freak snow, a furious freak show of Mother Nature's complete disregard for seasonal boundaries. The winds howled like cattle under hot irons and snow obscured the roads, drifting high like homeless hobos from town to town. With the heater blasting hot air, The Green Machine idled and shuddered in the fierce wind as we sat stranded for hours. When the weather finally broke, we left Flagstaff in a furious flurry, forcing the hand of fate, falling into the future of our making.

"Let's go see the big hole," I shouted as I drove north on a whim toward the Great Rift in the Earth. "We still have a few hundred left from my royalties...I say we use some of it to get a nice room somewhere. We've been on the road for a long time, and we're tired, hungry, and we stink. A shower and a real bed will feel damn good."

"You may stink," Ted said with a smug grin. "I do not."

"Oh, baby," Tessa said. "You are mistaken."

147

At the Grand Canyon we got the last available room at the Inn, just one step ahead of Joseph and Mary. I offered first shot at the bathroom to Ted and Tessa, and they made several abbreviated attempts at a long, hot shower with water that went too quickly cold. Ted trimmed his goatee, Tessa shaved her legs and even her armpits, while I sat on the bed and watched a turned-off TV.

"Your turn," Tessa announced as she pranced from the bathroom.

"Well, don't you two clean up nice," I said with a whistle. "Tessa, did you wash the stink off Ted?"

"I got the outside," she said. "But can't do a damn thing about the inside."

Tessa was wrapped in a towel, and Ted smacked her bottom playfully. She giggled and flashed him, then threw in a dose of Rimbaud, "Then you'll feel a tickle on your cheek…a little kiss like a crazed spider fleeing down your neck."

"Hey, Brunky," Ted said with a wink. "Maybe you should take a good looonnng shower now. And take your time in there…don't rush out on our account."

"I get the message, Teddy."

The spray from the showerhead smacked my face like a fountain of truth on my life of lies. I lathered up and scrubbed my skin the way my mother used to scrape the bottom of a pork chop skillet. The water turned ice cold and I stared straight into the stream and cursed it.

I got out of the shower and studied my reflection in the mirror over the sink, sinking ever deeper into the morass of my stinking life. *How fitting to be here at the world's biggest hole in the ground,* I whispered. I felt as though I'd been three nights strapped to a wind-rocked tree, pierced by the cruel spears of misfortune. I was swinging like Roger Miller's pendulum do, wildly back and forth, rattled, erratic, and stumbling along a path that grew ever more unfamiliar and frightening. *Something's got to change.*

I smeared lemon-lime Barbasol shaving cream on my face and attacked my wild whiskers with the razor. On a shocking whim, I held out my eight-inch length of goat chin hair, placed the blade at its roots, and cut with no hesitation, no pomp nor ceremony, and no regard for the consequences. Years of growth, my trademark facial hair, fell loosely into the sink. Numb, with no remorse, I stared down at the strands of blue hair lying limply in the basin like strands of time in the sink of my mind. It reminded me of the words of the poet, Michael Crisp, about a majestic tree cut down in its prime:

> *Sixty years of living, growing;*
> *Sixty seconds marks its going,*
> *Year upon and year and ring upon ring,*
> *Now someone buys a wooden thing.*

A strange, clean-shaven man stared back at me from the battered mirror in the dim light. Purplish half-moons rested uneasily beneath his eyes, and his pupils had tiny, black flames but no sparkle. His face was boyish, yet creased with long lines of longing and anguish.

It seemed as though I had forever been saying goodbye to and attempting to part with this sorrowful someone that I was, a sad figure partially obscured by and

149

waving meekly from behind pulled-back curtains at the window. Yet, I always found him waiting anxiously to rejoin me around every bend in the road, and always staring back at me from every mirror. He and I were forever waking to unaccomplished dreamscapes, regretful handshakes, hollow-eyed heartaches, brazen band mates, and sinfully serpentine sand snakes who lay curled in well-crafted lairs of lies.

I gazed into the glass and inspected my naked body – wiry at best, skeleton-like at worst. My limbs were too thin and my stomach hugged my spine, the result of two years on the road, too little food, and enough anger and alcohol to fuel a death diet. I had been in metabolic meltdown for too long and my ribs testified loudly to that truth.

"We're going to the bar & grill," Tessa said, knocking at the door, startling me, "Put some clothes on and come with us."

"I'm staying in the room," I replied.

"No, you're not."

"Yes, I am."

"I swear to God," she said loudly. "If you don't get dressed and come with us, I will break this door down and beat the living shit out of you."

I saw myself smile at myself in the mirror. Tessa was one person who could still have that effect on me. But I could tell by her tone that she would not take no for an answer, and I suspected from what I'd seen of her martial arts abilities that she and her black belt could probably fulfill her threat. I didn't have the energy to argue and I didn't want to fuel her ire. I joined them at the bar and grill.

"Oh, my dear God," Tessa exclaimed when she saw me, "You shaved it off! You shaved it all off. Why?"

"And I was just starting to get used to it," Ted said with a grin.

Tessa was staring a hole through me, "I want to know what possessed you to do that. And I want to know right now."

"It was a whim. I thought it might help me pick up girls," I said sarcastically.

"Bullshit," Ted said. "Where is it? You didn't throw it away, did you?"

"Actually, it's folded up in my pocket."

"I say we glue that thing back on," Ted suggested.

Tessa rubbed my face. "My, but you do have quite the baby face when you're clean shaven. Maybe it *will* help your love life."

I did vodka shots with PBR chasers at the middle-America, white-bread bar while Ted and Tessa engaged in a variety of social activities. They played pool with two young cheese-heads, quarter-bounce with some Longhorns from UT, and darts with a young couple from Connecticut who'd taken a break from the corporate world to come gaze into the Great Chasm. I observed stoically from my stool, half-heartedly raising a glass to their victories and shrugging sympathetically at their losses.

A red-haired woman with long nails and finger-less gloves leaned on the bar beside me. She wasn't your conventional redhead - her hair was dark crimson, the color of blood when it's spilled. She was sharp and shapely in a short scarlet skirt and tight white top, and wore Mary Janes on her feet with white socks pulled up high like a southern sorority girl in training. Her eyes were jade – exactly the shade Emily's had been – and that immediately drew my attention.

"You don't like games?" she said, holding her glass of Tanqueray at eye level between us, peering seductively over the top of it, and swirling the drink slowly so that the ice clinked like distant bells in a tiny kingdom.

"I choose my games more carefully than most."

"Hmmm," she said with increasing interest, setting her glass daintily on the bar. She leaned close to me with a conspiratorial air about her, and looked around the room with me as though seeing it through my eyes rather than hers.

"You're tired of all this, aren't you?" She didn't wait for an answer. She didn't need answers – she already had them.

"I know exactly what you're thinking," she said. "You're thinking that couple in the corner is poorly matched, that she's probably frigid and he has a cock like a horse's leg. And you think those fat guys over there screaming at the ballgame on television would keel over dead halfway through a forty-yard dash if forced to get up off their fat asses and run one. And you think the guy at the end of the bar is eyeing you."

She leaned in even closer and whispered in my ear, "And, you think you know more about life than anyone else in the room. How am I doing so far?"

I smirked slightly, barely perceptible, but she saw it.

"My, aren't you a talker," she said, grinning like a cat. "I bet you've been through some serious shit."

"I've seen more shit than a sewer," I said.

"You know what they say: *what doesn't kill you makes you stronger.*"

"Correction," I said. "What doesn't kill you only delays the inevitable."

"Oh, and a great sense of humor, too. I like that in a man."

She ordered another drink and then turned back to me. "Have you ever been with a redhead?" she asked.

"Are you naturally red or do you get it from a bottle?"

She slowly slid the front of her skirt down a couple inches to reveal the top edge of a neatly trimmed, narrow, vertical line of red hair down below. I felt a stirring in my loins, something that hadn't happened in a long while. I'd been with no other woman since Emily died and hadn't even once considered it.

"So you've really had your heart broken, haven't you." she said, more as a statement than a question.

"Into very tiny pieces," I said.

"Do you know why there are broken hearts?"

I did not respond and she pressed on, "Because that's the nature of life – everything breaks eventually. *Everything*, including hearts. And things that break need someone to fix them. Broken hearts keep love in business."

She led me outside into the cool night moonlight, and for some unknown reason, I did not resist. We wound our way across the parking lot through rows of silent sedans and sleeping SUV's. Hand in hand, we let our feet do the talking, walking toward a moment that mightily muddled my mind.

She slid the key slowly into the slot in the door and pulled it back out, then repeated the process with jade eyes laughing in the lunar light. Once we were inside, a girlish pout cleverly commandeered her lips, but the rest of her body had a mind of its own. She walked a fine line between erratic and erotic as she cast her clothes recklessly about the room, depicting a design of disarray, much like that of my life, until her young, smooth body was as bare as my soul.

Every time I tried to speak, she kissed me, lapping up my language, literally licking the words from my mouth to hers with her wet tongue. She moved as the speed of light at absolute zero, with an abandon that belied her cunning. The room was spinning and so was my head,

153

but counter to one another such that time seemed to stand still, like compound circles in conflicting elliptical orbits spinning to the power of all and none.

She catapulted against me, forcing me to the bed, and poured herself onto me like hot syrup on pancakes with crimson nipples, maple skin, and buttery thighs. She was sensually decadent like a Sybarite descendant, pressing her voodoo spear against my throat as she slid herself down upon me and began to grind.

"What's your name," I rasped.

"What does it matter?" she asked.

"I don't know," I said. "I just want to know who you are."

She changed positions and took me in her mouth.

"Oh, God," I cried out, writhing with her in feverish ecstasy.

She swung her body around until her genitals were positioned over my face, permitting me access and pleading that I reciprocate in kind to her oral performances. She lifted her mouth from me long enough to say, "My name's Emily. What's yours?"

I froze, wondering if I'd heard correctly, fearing that I had. "Wh-what?!"

"Emily," she repeated, "My name's Emily. What's yours?" and then slid her lips back upon my hardness.

I gazed through a haze of crazed bewilderment into her gentle folds of pink, now dripping rhinestones upon my lips.

I roared something indiscernible and cast her from me. She fell awkwardly from the bed and cried out in pain and anger. I stood in the middle of the spinning hotel room, clenching and unclenching my fists, muttering to myself, "Why? Why does my life always have to be so screwed all to hell?"

I turned toward the woman in the floor, shook my head in resignation to my miserable fate, and laughed like a fool. "I have all the luck," I said. "Emily. Your name is Emily. What are the odds?"

"What the hell is wrong with you?!" she screamed in furious confusion. "Keep away from me, you damn psycho!"

We were sweating, panting, and painting an unwanted portrait of unvarnished pain. We exchanged soliloquies of silence, breathing hard, sharing the stage for a long moment until the glare of the spotlights became unbearable. I grabbed my clothes and ran, never looking back.

Ted, Tessa, and I drove for days in wide circles around the Four Corners, trying tangents, pursuing parallels, and pushing perpendicular to a purpose. We did things we'd never done before, simply because we'd never done them before. We got drunk as dingoes in the desert, pricked our fingers on prickly pear, bought weed on the reservation and smoked it beneath the water tower in Tuba City.

Chewing on buffalo jerky, I gunned the Green Machine, and we rumbled through an incomparable display of hackberry, chokeberry, iron oxide, manganese, riparian streams, and red rock monoliths. Sandstone alcoves peered one-eyed at russet-colored buildings and clapboard houses hedged about by junked flatbed trucks, discarded tires, and piles of old fence posts.

Sagebrush smiled, cactus cackled, and locoweeds laughed as we roared uninhibited across uninhabited miles. I leaned forward at the wheel, my hair wild, my mouth working hard on the jerky, eyes flashing back and forth from windshield to rear view to side mirror as though we were being pursued. I couldn't help thinking that Ted was perhaps Kerouac to my Dean as we rode mad and wild on the road like misplaced beatniks out of sync and out of time. Treading dangerously along the fringes of my unconscious mind, I spewed forth a stream-of-consciousness lyric:

One forty-seven a.m. in the morning,
Got a big crazy dream
Marching through my head,
Right shoe, left foot, javelin, shot-put,
There's some kind of evil lurking in my bed,
Take a hot shower on a cold summer day,
Driving my Yugo on the green green grass,
Put a little vodka in my Perrier,
I'm a window pane with a broken glass,
Centuries of sediment,
Wonder where my edge went,
Buy a vowel, take a sip,
Atomic weight of skyy drip,
Here we go again, here we go again,
Singing hey, hey, oomm soppa day yay…

I hadn't slept much in days, as well as I could recall, and I had no plans to. I pulled off somewhere in the San Juan Mountains, and Ted and I played a drinking game of our own inebriated creation – something we called a cigarette race. It was quickly conceived by our rapidly deteriorating minds, and there were two simple rules. Smoke a cigarette as quickly as possible. Last one done had to chug.

When I was totally wasted, I shot holes in a road sign with my pistol and cursed the darkness. I was not good company.

Tessa decided to tread on dangerous ground. "You know what, Brunky…I'm sick of your bad attitude. You're getting crazier and more bitter by the day."

"By the hour," Ted added.

I gave him a dirty look.

"Think about it," Tessa continued. "Here we are, traveling America, living in the moment and on the edge. This should be a glorious adventure for us, Brunky, the greatest time of our lives, but it's almost like you're determined to ruin it with your bitterness. Don't you see that?"

"Bitterness is all I have."

Tessa grabbed my arm and shook me. "No, that's not true. You have *us*. Ted and I have stayed by your side through everything, and we always will."

I sighed and rubbed my hands hard over my whiskered face and aching head. "I know...I know...but I don't know what to say, Tess. I wish I could tell you that I've got things all figured out. I wish I could clear my head and wipe the pain from my heart. But I can't."

A lonely silence fell over the three of us like stink on a wet dog. We huddled together and shivered in the cold as the moonlight cast shape-shifting shadows upon the San Juan Mountains.

"Ah, the hell with it," I said finally. "Let's dance."

Like ballistic banderilleros, we turned up the volume on the van's stereo system and did the tarantella and the cha-cha to "Ring of Fire" until we collapsed in an inebriated trance. I felt like a tattoo in search of a body, like a shadow seeking a light, like algae on a narwhal tusk, like a dog with no bone to pick with anyone but me.

Dreams wavered on the fringes of my tortured mind as shooting stars shot holes in the sky. No one spoke and no one heard the end of things approaching.

Even my mother was silent.

Too much booze,
Not enough sleep;
Too much lose,
Not enough keep.

-- Michael Crisp

Ted, Tessa and I headed east again and tumbled into Texas from the top, crossing that intangible line in the prairie grass between Lone Star and Sooner. It was the same type of indefinable transition as the one I crossed daily between the man I was and the one I wished I'd been. I dreamed as we drove through the desolation of widely scattered, dead or dying Texas towns with ramshackle trailers, burned-out shells of cinderblock buildings, crumbling roofs, faded signs that read "Calves For Sale," and yard sales where hopeless wares – corduroy pants, battered bird baths, plastic lawn ornaments of the Virgin Mary, floor model TVs, and assorted ceramic knick-knacks – were displayed in disarray for a ghost market bereft of buyers.

From Perryton to Amarillo to Childress, tiny towns clung to brown dirt as we ventured through, sometimes hugging, sometimes skirting the Burlington Northern Railroad line. The Green Machine labored faithfully – *my father would be proud of her* – beneath a steel blue curtain as we explored the northern expanses of the lonely Lone Star State.

For many weeks, most of my energy and attention had been focused on Emily – missing her, yet also torturing myself about her mysterious journal entries. Memories of my mother had been held at bay, pushed into the back of my mind where they lurked and waited. But the back of my mind had crept closer to the front – limbic stalking frontal lobe – and my mother made a resurgence in Texas. She started whispering to me and I kept shushing her.

"What are you doing?" Ted asked.

"Shushing my mother," I answered.

"Oh," Ted said.

"Do you believe in ghosts?" I asked.

"Only slightly more than I believe in Big Foot," Ted answered.

"Then I guess you'd be very skeptical of a Big Foot ghost."

Ted said, "A *what?*"

Tessa suddenly became interested in our conversation. She pulled off her headphones and said excitedly, "Did somebody see a Big Foot?"

"When people die they come back as ghosts," I said. "So what do ghosts come back as when they die?"

For a moment, there was only the sound of Michelins grooving on the lonely, sunbaked strip of pavement that cut through the middle of Texas.

"Sheets," Tessa suggested after considerable thought.

Even though her response made little sense, I found it exceedingly humorous and laughed uncontrollably; causing the van to swerve from side to side on the two-lane road.

Panicked, Tessa shouted, "Whoa, whoa, get a grip!"

But, like a fool, I was laughing too hard at that particular moment.

Ted reached across to grab the wheel in an attempt to straighten us out.

"I don't need your help," I shouted indignantly, pushing his hand away. "I've got it under control."

"No, you don't," he argued, grabbing the steering wheel again.

"Hit the brakes!" Tessa shouted from the back.

I looked up just in time to see a large, white chicken slam into the windshield.

"What the hell?!" I hit the brakes hard and we slid to a stop on the side of the road.

No one said a single word as we climbed out of the van and gathered around our fallen, feathered friend. She did not look well at all.

Finally, Tessa said, "Colonel Sanders is going to be pissed at you."

"Maybe it's just stunned," I suggested.

"It is dead," Ted said.

"Damn, I'm sorry, little fella," I said, bending down to scoop up our victim.

Suddenly the chicken squawked, flapped its wings crazily, and flew up into my face, knocking me on my ass in the dirt.

We laughed like there was no tomorrow, laughed until our sides ached.

Ted, who rarely used curse words, said, "*Son of a bitch.* How did that chicken survive that impact?"

"We have witnessed a poultry miracle, my friends," I said, tears streaming down my face, hands raised to the heavens. "I have seen the light – there is a God!"

Something snapped in my brain as we leaped back into the Green Machine, and I pushed the gas pedal to the floor. Still weeping, I was soaring toward a flat horizon that sent my spirit vertical. I was behind the wheel, above the fray, ahead of the curve, and beyond myself with an

excitement born of hopelessness.   I'd gone behind the
curtain and seen my Wizard.   I'd pushed the envelope and
mailed myself a glowing letter of recommendation.   I
didn't know what lay ahead, but I knew I was going there.

At a thrift store in Amarillo, Tessa paid a quarter for a tiny ceramic Chihuahua wearing pink boots. Ted had a jalapeno burger at El Jaciliete, and I drank an early morning Schlitz with a man I'd never see again. A bright orange sign at the First Independent Congregational Church of Christ proclaimed: "Jesus Celebrated Here!"

"I was not aware that Jesus ever paid a visit to Amarillo," Ted said.

"Joseph Smith said he saw him in Salt Lake City," I replied. "Guess he could've been here too."

"Probably came for the jalapeno burger," Ted suggested.

We resisted the urge to rent three rooms of furniture for only $29.95 at Ike's Instant Rental. Likewise, we chose not to give blood at the Plasma Biological Center, or to wait around for Tuesday night Bingo at the American Legion Post. The open land was calling my name as clearly as a poker player with an open-ended straight draw calls for the flop.

I purchased a Texas road map at a gas station from an Aggie cheerleader who was sucking on an Icee and wearing short shorts, cowboy boots and a halter top. She could have sold fire to the Devil.

I leaned over the counter and whispered to her in my sexiest voice, "You should come with us. We have a cooler full of bologna."

163

She looked at me like I was a fly on her Texas barbeque. Deadpan, she said, "I prefer salami."

I shrugged, "Your loss."

"Loser," she mumbled as we went out the door.

Outside, Tessa took my arm and said, "That was smooth, Brunky, real smooth."

We returned to the van and I studied the map while feasting on bologna, pork rinds and beer, the preferred meal of my father. "Ah, yes, almighty bologna! King of the Meats," I proclaimed.

"What's with you and bologna?" Tessa asked. "Don't you ever get tired of it?"

"Trust me," Ted said. "The answer is no. I've known Brunky for years and he has never grown weary of a slab of bologna between two slices of fresh white bread."

"Maybe because it's tied to the only good memory I have of my parents," I suggested. "I was seven years old and we'd gone to visit relatives for a few days. It was a long trip; we were in the car for hours and I was starving. Not much was open in those days on old country roads late on a Sunday night. But finally, Dad found this little mom and pop store, and we got a loaf of bread and a stack of fresh, sliced bologna from their deli. It was the best thing I've ever tasted in my entire life."

"Funny how something like that can stick with us forever," Tessa said.

"Yeah, it was a good hour or two," I said with a sad smile. "For some reason, my mother and father weren't angry or arguing that night. It was the only time I ever felt an inkling of what it might be like to be part of a real family, a happy family."

"All because of bologna," Tessa said, smiling in her usual, adorable manner.

"All because of bologna," I repeated.

"Alright, listen up. I have a plan. I know where we're going," I said, pointing to the map. "Here – the Prairie Dog Town Fork of the Red River."

"The what?" they asked in unison. "Why?"

"Because I like the sound of it."

They made faces at each other as the Green Machine's 351 Windsor engine roared to life and carried us toward a deeper wilderness. The railroad line ran east-west, directly through the center of Amarillo, splitting it in half right down the middle, a sternum through the ribs of civilization, and we followed it into the plains.

"We're going out in the country!" I screamed. "Yee haw!"

"We're going to the country? Then what, pray tell, do you call *this*?" Ted asked.

"Ah, my friend, this is a bustling metropolis compared to where we're headed. We're going where the bed bugs are big as coyotes, and the coyotes are big as oxen."

"And how big are the oxen?" Tessa giggled and mussed my hair. *Damn, Ted is a lucky man.*

I put *Harvest* in the cassette player and cranked it up to match my amped-up neurons and cracked-up brain. "Are you ready for the country?" I shouted along with Neil. "Because it's time to go! Toss me some more of that jerky, Teddy boy. I miss my goat chin. Why'd you let me shave it? And you call yourselves my friends," I said in mock derision.

I observed my face in the mirror and did an about face. "Hell, no," I said. "I don't miss it. I look damn good like this. *Damn good.* Good enough to eat." My conversation had kicked into a reckless hyper-stream-of-consciousness mode.

"I still can't get used to seeing you without those long strands of hair hanging from your chin," Tessa said. "It was so much a part of you."

"He had it almost as long as I have known him," Ted said, "Hell, I was there when he first grew it. I'm the one who named it the 'goat chin'. I think I should get to keep the clippings as a memento."

"My right side tingles like it's buzzing with exotic electricity," I said, ignoring Ted's request for the hair in my pocket, pulling up my shirt to look for signs of sizzling skin. "Damn, I miss my guitar. Why did you let me leave it behind? Why didn't you stop me?"

"We tried," Ted and Tessa chimed together.

"You did what you felt you had to do," Ted said. "Do not beat yourself up about it."

"Too late. The beating has begun."

"Let's get you another one," Tessa suggested.

I shook my head dismissively and moved on to a new topic in my ongoing helter-skelter fashion.

"Did you know Emily and I were born on the same day in the same hospital?" I asked. "It's true. Not the same year, of course. Our mothers gave birth in the same hospital room. Now, that's freaking star-crossed, by God. Old Will Shakespeare didn't have nothin' on us." I continued to shift mental gears and jump subjects like a crackhead kangaroo.

"I killed my mother," I said, stumbling and tumbling through the narrow hallways of my sleep-deprived and over-alcoholed mind. "There is so much you don't know about me...so much no one knows."

Ted and Tessa did not respond, waiting to see if this was just one more absurd statement along a distorted path leading nowhere.

"I weaved in and out of *double-trouble mister* in the ransacked rubble and busted bubble of my childhood," I continued. "And then I put the metaphorical gun in her hand. Was I her angel of mercy or her executioner? Did I ease her suffering or did I flip the switch to her demise? It's all a matter of perspective, isn't it?"

"What in the hell are you talking about, Brunky?" Ted said.

"I thought your mother died of cancer," Tessa said. "God rest her soul."

"Killing someone is not as simple as it sounds," I went on, ignoring their comments. "It has far-reaching implications and reverberations with tentacles that coil more deeply within you as the years go by. And I can tell you this with certainty – killing is not as easy as depicted on television, and it's certainly not as common. Being a murderer actually puts you in a very small percentile of the population."

I moved my hands from the steering wheel and put them to my puffed out chest, pretending as though I was pulling outward on make-believe suspenders with exaggerated pride. "Look at me," I said. "Now I'm really *somebody*. I'm a killer!"

"Brunky," Ted said, putting one hand uneasily on the wheel, "Perhaps we should stop and stretch our legs. Let me drive for a while. You have not slept much in the last few days, and maybe you are not thinking clearly."

"Even more exclusive," I shouted with grand hand gestures for added emphasis, "is the Matricide Club! I'm a card-carrying member! Riddle me this, Batman: how many people can truly say they killed their own mother?"

167

Ted moved his hand from the wheel and placed it gently on my shoulder, a gesture that was partly an attempt at consolation and partly meant to humor me. "Relax, Brunky, we'll get through this together," he said. "Now, seriously, we need you to study the map so that we can find this river of yours. How about you let me drive for a while?"

"I'm driving," I said sternly. "I'm driving till I find the fucking Prairie Dog Town Fork of the fucking Red River smack dab in the middle of fucking Texas."

I turned abruptly off Route 70 onto a crumbling stretch of baking pavement with a ghostlike yellow line down the middle. As *Harvest* played on, Neil Young reminded us of the damage done, a little part of it in everyone. "That's right, Neil...that's what I'm saying," I said, nodding my head vigorously, failing to see the vulture perched atop a faded road sign.

"Most of the things we do in life really don't matter much in the grand scheme of things," I said, turning toward Ted. "But some things are monumental and they change everything, forever. And you can't erase them, and you can't rewind them like you can this cassette we're listening to."

"I suppose that is true," Ted said.

"My mother was a bitch," I continued. "And she saved her greatest evil for the final act in her life. She spread these dark shadows over me that have haunted me ever since."

I adopted a more demeaning tone and began casting aspersions like eggs lobbed toward awnings on Halloween night. "Oh, and everybody thinks they've got the solution, don't they? Buddhists say you can meditate your problems away, release your pain into the universe. Christians tell you to lay it at the feet of Jesus, put it under the blood, and walk away with a clear conscience. High and mighty psychologists promise that therapy will free you from your demons. But don't you believe a word of any of it. It's all bullshit. You're never free. *Never.*"

I turned off the paved road and followed a dirt trail through a barren land of stocky sagebrush, jagged ravines, dry creek beds, and sandstone outcroppings. The sun threw red ocher, umbra, and realgar onto the day's curtain as the Green Machine battled its way over the rough terrain.

"We're almost there," I said, hanging my head out the window. "I can feel it, by God, I can smell it."

Excitement gave way to a sense of dread as we dug deeper into desolation. It reminded me of Dylan's *Highway 61 Revisited* which, like *Harvest*, was one of only a handful of tapes about which I'd cared enough to bring on our journey. I put it in the player, rolled all the windows down and blasted "Desolation Row" out into the translucent Texas troposphere. It was a glorious moment as we approached the precipice of possibility, the cusp of crisis, and the dusk of disillusionment.

I guided my father's Green Machine up a rocky knoll at a thirty degree angle with underbody scraping bottom and the wheels spinning, kicking dirt, and throwing rocks like protons hurled from a particle accelerator. We reached the top and sat in a promontory cloud of grasshoppers and dust in the late afternoon sun.

Stretched out below us was the Prairie Dog Town Fork of the legendary Red River. Or, at least, what was left of it. Mostly dry riverbed, it was not quite what I expected. There were no raging torrents, no dark, churning waters, and yet it was beautiful in its own minimalistic manner. There was a quilted pattern of red clay, grainy rock, and white silt and sand with a series of shallow puddles connected by wandering snakes of water. It behaved like a river that had nothing to prove.

We stepped out of the van and surveyed the glory from the knoll top. I left the stereo system powered, out of respect for the Master, to allow the epic "Desolation Row" to play its full eleven minutes and twenty-one seconds. I had vowed early in my life never to cut a song off short, and I was diligent in my application of the rule. I firmly believed and obeyed Robert Frost's teaching that we should never seek to silence any song, and certainly not a masterpiece.

"Are you certain this is it?" Tessa asked with a great deal of doubt.

"More certain than I've ever been about anything," I said.

"It must be a sight to behold after a downpour." Ted said.

"Yes, it's nearly dry now, but, my God, it's still magnificent. I've never seen anything like it," I said as I climbed down the hillside and lay on my back in the damp riverbed. I cupped handfuls of the moist red clay and smeared it gently on my cheeks, took off my grandfather's boots and felt it between my toes. Dylan's voice continued to ring out across the vast emptiness as twilight fell upon us. I felt like a rolling stone with the tombstone blues as we meditated under a million stellar eyes, and I was definitely a thin man.

"Emily used to put corn chips in her soup," I said to my friends. "Have you ever heard of that before?"

"Yeah, I remember that," Ted said. "She was quirky that way. Quirky good."

"Yeah, yeah," I said. "She was, wasn't she? Quirky...and perky...and she liked turkey...I'll have some more jerky, please." I laughed like a bipolar, manic-depressive idiot who'd had too many vodka shots with lack-of-sleep chasers.

"Something is happening here, but I'm not sure what it is," I said, quoting Dylan. "Hey, did you know I almost met him once?"

"Who?" Ted asked, "Dylan's Mr. Jones?"

"No, Dylan himself, backstage at some big show...I can't remember where we were...Cincinnati...maybe Detroit or Philly...hell, I don't know...but Dylan was there. He was like some supernatural ephemeral majestic mirage of misappropriated mystery--"

"Easy for you to say," Ted said.

"I was about to shake his hand, and he sorta looked through me and then disappeared." I slowly shook my head, remembering the scene; then picked up a rock and threw it at a vulture. "Asshole," I said. "Where does he get the right to treat people that way? It was like I didn't even exist to him. Maybe he was right. Maybe I don't exist at all."

"Perhaps not," Ted said. "Poe suggested we are all but a dream within a dream."

I turned my hand slowly before my face, studying it, trying to determine if I was real. "Yeah...yeah, I wonder about that sometimes..."

Tessa elbowed Ted and whispered, "You're not helping with comments like that, Einstein. We need to calm him down, get him thinking about something good."

She turned toward me and said, "Tell me more about Emily. I like hearing you talk about her. It's strange how someone I never met could mean so much to me. I want to know what she was really like."

"Truth is," I said very softly, "The real Emily, the regular Emily, when she wasn't overcome by the darkness of her fear and obsessions and addictions, was exactly like you – perfect."

The moment those words slipped from my lips I sucked in a breath sharply, hoping that the words would

171

be sucked back in as well. Tessa didn't flinch. She sat facing me in the silt of the riverbed, her legs pulled up tight to her chest, chin resting on folded arms. She studied me with damp eyes as the uncomfortable moment lingered in our midst.

"You think Tessa's perfect?" Ted laughed, defusing the tension. "Clearly, you don't know her very well."

"Hey, I'm way out of your league, loser," Tessa said, playfully pinching Ted's thigh. "I only hang out with you because I feel sorry for you."

"You're not planning to leave me for some tat artist or preacher boy, are you?" Ted asked, his limbs intertwined with hers. Tessa had once dated a young evangelist.

"No, baby," Tessa replied, running her fingers through Ted's hair. "I'm not leaving you for some run-of-the-mill preacher. The Pope, yes. A Cardinal or a Bishop, maybe. But not for some weird-ass, tongues-speaking, snake-handling, backwoods evangelist."

"Ah, true love," I said.

We turned Bob off and let the sounds of the wasteland serenade us as night fell. The scene was serene and surreal, the moment magic, and we were as far from humanity as we could hope to be.

I lay on my back in the damp sand and whispered, "Emily had a faint scar like a crescent moon along her right cheekbone. It only added to her allure, somehow making her even more beautiful and attractive, as if she boldly bore the marks of childhood trauma and past life tribulations and victories."

"How did she get the scar?" Tessa asked.

"She told me that when she was a little girl, her father cut her with a broken bottle."

"Damn," Tessa said. "What the hell is wrong with people? I'll never understand how someone can mistreat a child."

"Takes all kind of scum to make a pond," Ted said.

"Emily was a great poet," I continued, lost in my memories. "Of course, that was one of the things that drew me to her. She dipped her pen in a well of wonder and mixed morsels of melancholy with tidbits of tainted tenderness. Sometimes a stream of consciousness like a bullet train, sometimes like Emily Dickinson on a bad hair day, she had a way of baring her soul to express the brokenness of every child who's ever been abandoned, and every lover who's ever sought to fit a round love in a square heart."

Dreamily, I continued to reminisce as the shadows stretched into pale night. "You know, it's funny the things you remember. Emily's eyelashes were long and delicate, like no one else I've ever seen. And her lips…her lips were the softest shade of pink on earth, maybe heaven, too. God, I used to just sit and stare at her sometimes…"

Ted and Tessa had huddled together under a blanket as the night grew cool, and they held one another a little tighter as I spoke, absorbing every sad syllable, no doubt sharing a similar thought – each fearing what they'd do without the other.

I laughed sadly to myself with ironic images twirling in my brain like misbegotten parasols in the past.

We climbed back into the safety and shelter of the van where Ted and Tessa bound themselves together in a sleeping bag and drifted off to a place I could no longer find, and believed I never again would. Instead, even in my great weariness, I trudged along the border of sleep without ever truly crossing over, like a fearful swimmer who interminably paces the water's edge, dips a toe in, but never quite musters the courage to plunge. I was being kept awake by my own somnolence.

The spirits of my mother and Emily hovered above me, casting claustrophobic chains upon me inside the van, whispering words of woe, incessantly murmuring things I could not quite interpret. The moonlight poured through the window like the watery truth on my flame. All my life, I'd unknowingly put my faith in serpents and vultures, and I'd been blind-sided by my own misguided, short-sighted foolishness. No one could shoulder the burden of blame but me.

I slipped quietly out of the van with a bottle of vodka and wandered the wasteland with the moonlight flinging eerie shadows upon my homeless face. Ancient spirits of the Kichai, Kiowa, and Wichitas murmured in Caddoan, reached up from the soil, and tugged at my pant legs as I wobbled half-drunk where bison once roamed. The prairie wind pushed hard at me in the darkness, but I pushed back. That was a good sign, I suppose, all things considered.

We were frying bacon and brewing coffee over an open fire when we spotted a figure approaching in the distance.

"Strange to see someone out here in the middle of nowhere," Ted observed.

"Well, *we're* out here," Tessa said, grinning. "So I guess it's not *all* that strange."

The man was not running, but he moved toward us at a rapid, steady pace, sometimes disappearing and reappearing as he followed the contours of the land. He was a large man with very dark skin and a shaved head, and he carried himself with steely determination. When he reached us he stopped abruptly and spoke.

"My name is Omo. My vehicle broke down many miles away and I began to walk. I became lost and have been wandering for two days now. I smelled your food. I am very hungry."

Tessa jumped up and handed him a plate and a cup of coffee. "I'm Tessa," she said. "Please sit down. You're welcome to join us."

"You have my eternal gratitude," Omo said as he wolfed down the food. "I will spend every waking hour seeking a way to repay you."

Is he being sincere or a smartass?

"Where are you from?" Tessa asked. "Your accent is very striking."

"Currently, I reside in red rock country. Arizona, that is. But I hail from Brazil where friends are like unicorns, and enemies are as thick as flies. My father was a Moro guerrilla and my mother was not of this world. She was a visitor from another planet." Omo smiled widely to reveal a large mouthful of bright white teeth. "Oh, I kid you."

"About which part?" I asked.

"Do you believe in extraterrestrials?" Omo answered with a question.

Simultaneously, I responded with a hearty *Yes* and Ted uttered a very skeptical *No*.

Tessa smiled and said, "So, your dad was a gorilla and your mom was an alien. Sounds like a great plot for a movie."

Omo's smile was disarming, almost too pleasant to fit him. "Not the kind of gorilla you are thinking, sweet girl – a Moro, a guerilla fighter in our land long ago. But you are correct: my life would most certainly make a four-star movie, something between a black comedy and a horror film, I presume."

"Okay," I said very slowly, uncertain about pursuing that topic, and choosing instead to change the subject. "What made you decide to leave Brazil and come to America?"

"Grand adventure and danger, my young man friend! If a motto were mine, that would be it. I wearied of old challenges; I crave new ones. I refuse to breathe for nothing. Do you understand what I am saying?"

I locked eyes with Omo and none of the four of us spoke for a long moment. Finally, I nodded and said, "Yes, I most certainly do."

Thunder rumbled ominously and shook the ground beneath us.

"Uh, oh," Tessa said, pointing to the west. "Looks like a storm coming."

"And coming quickly," Ted said.

Lightning splintered a tree and rain rushed upon us as though Almighty God had decided it was time for *The Great Flood: The Sequel.* We grabbed our things and tumbled into the safety of the Green Machine as the storm raged around us.

We drank and smoked and told stories until nightfall. Omo was a mesmerizing, almost other-worldly sort of man. I guess he took after his mother.

June 19, 1978

The rain was past, the stars were brilliant, and it was cold on the high Texas plains at two o'clock in the morning. Ted and Tessa were breathing softly, wrapped snugly together in a sleeping bag in the rear section of the van.

Quietly, I crept between the captain's chairs in the front seeking a blanket and a fresh drink. As I did, Omo slid quickly into the driver's seat and turned the key in the ignition of the Green Machine. It hummed softly.

"What are you doing?" I whispered, turning back toward him, alarmed. "I thought you were asleep."

"I admire your most unusual vehicle. I merely wanted to hear how she ran, see if the engine purred. And she does, she most certainly does."

"Yeah, my father poured his--"

Before I could finish, Omo said, "I want to see how she runs. May I?" He did not wait for an answer; he pressed the accelerator to the floor and the Green Machine roared and jumped violently forward.

"What...where are we going?" Tessa mumbled softly from deep within the sleeping bag.

The van shook and slid, bounced and jerked, as it scraped up and down hills and over rocks, gullies, mesquite, and clumps of sagebrush in the blackness. The van's headlights peered timidly ahead, shooting puny arrows of light into a quiver full of darkness.

Stunned, I lost my footing and fell to the floorboard. "What the hell are you doing, Omo?!"

"Adventure, my young friend," he shouted, as he weaved the van sharply from side to side.

Climbing out of the sleeping bag and trying unsuccessfully to keep his balance, Ted shouted from the back, "What's happening, Brunky? What's wrong?"

"Stop the van, Omo," I yelled. "You can't see where you're going. Stop now!"

He ignored me and I *knew* for sure we were in trouble. I scrambled to get to one of my guns, planning to put it to his head and make the bastard stop. Or blow his freaking brains out if need be.

But the ravine was waiting for us, mouth gaping, hematite teeth shimmering along sandstone gums. The van shot out over the edge and for a brief moment we were lost in space, suspended in mid-air, dangling at the end of a quickly closing noose. Then the Green Machine slammed face-first into red rock, crushing the grill, smashing the windshield, and we began to tumble back end over front end, an automotive head over heels, down the ravine toward oblivion. As we fell, somewhere along the way, Omo somehow pushed opened the driver's side door, flung himself out of the vehicle and disappeared into the darkness.

The earth battered the outside of the van like the hammer of Thor pounding a Dixie cup. Side panels and doors were ripped from their moldings and cast carelessly aside. Inside the van, pork rinds, cassettes, maps, and bottles seemed to hang in mid-air like weightless objects in the vacuum of deep space, floating, moving ever so slowly like caramel fingers through ice cream crevasses. I saw them as clearly as you see these words on paper – every detail and nuance, the fine print exposed in the roughest of moments. It was thirty seconds of breathless wonder, like thirty years of terror.

The Green Machine came to rest sitting straight up on its backside, wedged into the ravine bottom, as still as the subzero dead of a January night between War Ridge and Batoff Mountain. One single headlight had miraculously survived, and it peered dimly into the heavens toward Ursa Major, one paltry ray of terrestrial light beaming up toward an extra-terrestrial destination.

A cloud passed over the moon, and there was blood above the door frame, yet the angel of death entered anyway and waited. My head rested in shards of steel and glass, and I spoke in foreign tongues of Pentecostal flame, blame, and shame.

I drifted in and out of consciousness, and once, I could've sworn I saw a bloody Omo on a ridge just above the van, silhouetted against the moon, looking down at us. But then he was gone.

An odd gurgling sound emanated from somewhere in the darkness of the van behind and below me. I tilted my head and listened, fascinated and intrigued. It was all so very dreamlike. *What is that?* I wondered. *I have to find out.*

My eyes adjusted to the dark as moonlight and starlight peaked inside at the scene. I worked myself free and climbed through the scattered debris in the battered van. Tessa was at the bottom of it all, one of her legs pinned beneath the vehicle, crushed between metal and rock. She gasped with bloody lips, "Brunky, help me."

The moment hung as she clung to my neck, a wreck of crashing sorrow lashing forty stripes across both our bare, bloody souls.

"Hold on, Tessa," I pleaded. "I'm going to lift up one side of the van. When I do, you pull your leg out. Can you do that for me? Can you?"

Tessa nodded.

I pushed against the Green Machine with all my might, with strength I'd never known before; and when it tilted several inches on its backside, I shouted to Tessa, "Now, hurry! Pull yourself out!"

Tessa clawed at the dirt and cried out in pain as she dragged her mangled legs from beneath the wreckage. When she was clear of the van, I dropped it and collapsed in the red dirt.

The voice of reason in my head had been gagged and silenced, spurned like the angels in Sodom. My hands trembled and white spots danced before my eyes like idiopathic images of every "i" I'd ever dotted and every "t" I'd ever crossed. My neurotransmitters leaped across synapses like children tumbling in a school yard with not a single lesson learned. I was a carnivore loosed within a meat-packing plant, and great Danes were barking in my brain. All I could think before I lost consciousness was *I'm going to kill him. I'm going to kill Omo.*

When I woke, the sky was still black. *Was it the same night or another?* I comforted Tessa, gave her some water; and then, stumbling in the darkness, calling out his name, I went searching for my best friend.

I found Ted Mills on his side like a ship that listed, torn and twisted, his bloody locks on muddy rocks, choked and soaked in the liquid of life that had escaped from ruptured arteries and veins. His eyes were fixed firmly on nothing, having passed beyond the point of misery and fading into the moribund. He was long dead and eerie cold as a stone where he'd been thrown by the tumbling vehicle.

I screamed and fell to my knees.

A swirling wind from the southwest beat wildly around me, exceeded only by the swirling madness in my battered brain as I knelt beside my old friend's bloody body, and whispered, "I've wanted to tell you something,

Teddy...wanted to tell you what happened, what my mother made me do that day."

I cradled Ted against me and confessed all. Once it started, I couldn't stop it. The emotion I'd held inside for so very long finally poured out in a blazing torrent of terrible truth like bullets from an automatic weapon.

"My mother was in the hospital, Teddy, just like she'd been so many times before, and she was so sick and weak and tired of fighting the cancer...my father went to talk with the doctor while I stayed in the room with her. I was just a little boy, Teddy, just a kid...she told me to get her pills out of her bag in the closet, to bring them to her because she was too weak to get out of bed. What was I supposed to do, Teddy?" I clutched Ted's lifeless body tightly to my bosom and rocked back and forth with him as the words continued to pour from me.

"I found the bottle and gave it to her with some water. I was just a little kid doing what she asked, Teddy. I didn't know any better. She swallowed all the pills, Teddy, all of them...and just laid there smiling at me.

Then she took my hand and said, *you mustn't tell anyone about this...those doctors and nurses think I don't know what's best for me, but they're wrong...*and she squeezed my hand so hard it hurt... and she said, *mother does know what's best, doesn't she?* And I shook my head Yes...and she said, *Now put the bottle back in my bag and promise me that you won't ever tell anyone about this...*and I promised her, Teddy, I promised her...but why did she make me do it, Teddy, why? Why did I have to be the one to give her those pills?...I don't want to be the one..."

I stopped and brushed Ted's golden hair back from his lifeless eyes, and cradled him ever closer to me. "And then they told us to go home, and gave her some more medicines for pain and to help her sleep...they didn't know I'd just given her all those other pills. And she never woke up again. It's my fault, Teddy...I killed her. Emily's my fault too. And now you're gone. I should've stopped Omo. I should've...I'm so sorry, Teddy. Why can't I save anyone? Why does everyone always die around me?"

Like burning bastards in the bleak night, the sky shot bullets into the black, and Seven Sisters staggered like ballistic beacons lashed by the belt of Orion. An unseen heavenly orchestra began a dirge, a symphony of aching beauty and mournful majesty, with the cosmic conductor bringing in the oboes, calming the tympani, soliciting the somber strings. The repulsive odors of bowels, blood, vomit and death swirled about me as I lay down among the pasque-flowers and wept.

The sun rose and blinked like it was the first time it had ever seen a green van stuck in a ravine, sitting up on its backside in the High Plains of the Texas panhandle. It was a sanguine, sacred scene of sorrow, so still that movement seemed sinful. Yet I, ever the sinner, struggled slowly to my feet and surveyed the aftermath. Automotive panels, chrome scraps, articles of clothing, broken glass, two bodies – one dead, one resisting death – and a ceramic, pink-booted Chihuahua were scattered about the ravine. I stood still and silent for a long while, taking it all in, temporarily numb in the truest and most absolute sense of the word. I was spent. I did not talk to myself, pray, weep, or wail. I did not blink, did not think, yet did not shrink from what I beheld. My sensibilities had careened into that mean ravine as surely as had my father's Green Machine.

Finally, with calm detachment, and with the rising sun to my left as my marker, I grabbed a water bottle, picked up Tessa, and began to walk southeast. I knew that for her, time was of the essence, time was critical. I had to find help.

I did not see the vultures circling and, if I had, I would not have cared. I was past caring or feeling sorry. *Being sorry won't help a bit,* I told myself. *The only thing that will help now is to set things straight. I will kill him.* I walked away and did not look back.

Life is about doing what must be done, for this single day, for this very moment, and for this moment only.

Chop wood, carry water, as the master Roshi once said. Omo had become my wood and water. I would find him, chop him off at the source, and cast him into the fire. I would scoop him from the stream, haul him across the great river, and dump him into the depths of the dark sea.

Strengthened by rage and madness, I walked many miserable miles across the barren land, pushing on through terrain that was sometimes level, sometimes slashed by ravines like the one that had claimed us in the darkness. Tessa's breathing was shallow and labored, and from time to time, I spoke to her and put water on her lips, but she did not wake.

Soon I noticed my mother following us, several paces behind and to the right, shadowing us, and forever smiling that same hospital room smile. When I walked, she walked. When I stopped, she stopped.

"Stop following me!" I shouted. "Leave me alone."

The hours wore on as the earth wore on my feet as the sun bore on my head, and my immediate goal became my constant refrain – *Find a road, hitch a ride. Find a road, hitch a ride.*

Snakes and lizards scurried through the dirt like session players and I smiled precariously. *Find a road, hitch a ride.* I grew thirsty, then thirstier still. *Find a road, hitch a ride.*

After eight hours beneath the hot sun, my mother began to berate me anew. "You'll never find a road," she said.

Yes, I will.

"You'll die out here."

No, I won't.

"You fail at everything."

No, I don't.

"You're a murderer."

It wasn't my fault.

185

"You killed me."

And you might as well have killed me.

We engaged in this convoluted conversation until night collapsed upon me. Still I walked on. *Find a road, hitch a ride.*

In my madness, I saw Emily and me tumbling forth from the Fort Pitt Tunnel, spit out headlong into a barren wasteland where cacti loomed over me, casting their fearsome shadows toward an apocalyptic horizon. Behind every red rock, sweltering in desert heat, were the blackened, hollow eye sockets of maternal masochism, putrid flesh hanging loosely from darkened cheeks and chin. Perfectly aligned, razor-sharp teeth glimmered in my mother's smile as she shook her rotted head slowly from side to side.

"Just where is it you think you're going, young man?" my mother asked.

Find a road, hitch a ride.

"Pay attention when I talk to you."

Find a road, hitch a ride.

"You'll never make it."

Find a road, hitch a ride.

"You killed me and now you've killed your friends."

Burn in hell, mother, burn in hell.

I vomited in a patch of locoweed as my emotions churned and burned in my gut, and I became one part rage, one part sorrow, and fully vindictive, teetering dangerously on the fault line between a nihilistic chasm on one side, and the lofty peak of idealistic justice on the other.

When I stumbled over a cluster of rocks and fell into a prickly-pear plant, Tessa cried out in pain. As I lay there face down against the Earth, I felt it rushing along on its appointed path at a frantic pace, revolving and rotating through space while I held on for dear life, my fingers clawing into the dirt with handfuls of hurt. I pressed my ear to the ground and could hear the echoes of all those who'd gone before me and the portentous drumbeat of all those yet to come; marching, approaching, and pushing me aside in the process, urging me to quit the fight, to surrender and give up the ghost. But today would not be that day.

I struggled to my feet with Tessa in my arms, and began my familiar refrain once again: *Find a road, hitch a ride.*

Full-faced and wide-eyed, I stared into the abyss of a bitter, furious anger that had no rival in the history of mankind. No one else could know what I felt. No one could comprehend the depths of the rage that swallowed me whole. Cold is what comes to a crooked soul on the cusp of collapse. And I was very cold. My world had cracked the way the surface of a frozen pond cracks when you drop a cinderblock at its center. The fissures run from the point of impact, pushing farther across the surface of the unsuspecting ice, each one birthing new fractures, fingers of breakage reaching toward the edges in all directions, the rupture spreading exponentially with no way to halt it.

Vicious, thick-headed clouds suddenly intruded into the early morning Texas sky, with chins jutted forward in a vengeful pose, and they hung there like harbingers of certain doom wearing cruel stratospheric smiles. An angry, icy torrent scissored sideways against my gait, cold rocks of rain stinging my body like angry kamikaze hornets. The wind was ferocious and spokes of lightning wheeled down from heaven to earth. But I laughed as I walked, mouth open to the heavens, refreshed by the cold water as it washed the dried blood from my face and body. The storm went just as quickly as it came, and I spit at it in defiance as it moved away, daring it to come back.

At last I found a road waited patiently for me, lying snugly against the earth, a faded gray strip of pavement, now damp with rain. I followed it, walking east down the center line, certain that Route 83 was in my future. *Found a road. Now hitch a ride.*

For an hour, I saw not one single vehicle. Finally a beat-up pick-up approached, moving leisurely in the afternoon sun. Two Mexicans were driving a Japanese vehicle listening to British pop music and chasing the American Dream. I flagged them down and they stopped alongside me, flashing friendly smiles. Their hands were calloused, their skin leathered and dark, and their eyes even darker. They were hard-working men in a hard world.

"You need help?" the passenger asked, leaning out the window.

Stupid question.

"Yes, please. My friend...she's been hurt...real bad...I need to get her to a hospital."

The two men helped me lay Tessa in the back of the pickup and I cradled her head in my lap. "You're going to be okay, Tessa. Stay with me," I whispered as the old truck rattled and sputtered quickly down the highway.

In the bed of the pickup there were fence posts, a bag of cement, garden tools, and a very long, tall woman – probably 18 inches taller than me – stretched out flat on her back, her head resting on a rolled-up feed sack. I had been so intent on Tessa, that I'd paid her no mind. She was staring at me with big eyes wide, whites like fields of virgin snow.

"Will you...talk to...me?" she asked.

I studied the woman, pondering the odd question and her halting manner of speech. She was homely looking with a kind face, not entirely unattractive, with eyes set close together, and a wide-open, childlike smile.

"Will you...talk to...me?" she repeated.

"I don't feel very much like conversation," I replied.

"You...don't like...me?"

"I'm sorry...I'm just tired," I said.

"What...do you want to...talk about?" she asked.

I actually smiled, realizing that in some odd way, I'd found a kindred soul of sorts. She was as pitiful as me.

"What...happened to...your head?" she asked, pointing. "You...have blood...there."

I reached up instinctively and touched my scalp and face. I hadn't considered my possible injuries until that moment.

"I hurt...my head...once," the woman continued. She rose up on one elbow, pulled back her wind-blown, auburn hair, and pointed to a four-inch scar on the side of her head. "See...it?"

"Yes, I see it. How did it happen?"

"I hurt...my head," she repeated, as if that were explanation enough. I suppose it was.

"I was in...the army...one of the...first girls," she continued. "I was the...only girl...in my platoon." She smiled proudly and it brightened her face, though the smile came disjointed from her statement, making her appear like a bad actor struggling to synchronize lines with facial expressions. "I liked...being a soldier...but they said...I had to come...back home."

"I'm very sorry to hear that," I said.

"I hurt...my head," she repeated, putting her hands to her head as I had to mine. "I take...medicine..."

"Does it help?"

"Helps...I liked...the Army. They...taught me...good lessons...my... sergeant said...'*Hurry up and wait.*' Isn't...that funny?"

She paused and smiled her big goofy grin before continuing, "And…he said…'*If the enemy is in range, so are you*'. And…'*Be polite. Be professional. But have a plan to kill everyone you meet.*'"

"Your Sergeant gave excellent advice," I said.

The woman could recite military axioms flawlessly, yet normal conversation was enormously difficult for her. She reminded me of Mel Tillis, the famous country singer who stuttered when he talked but not when he sang, and for some reason I was overcome with great waves of compassion and sorrow for the woman. Why did I always seem drawn to the downtrodden dregs of humanity, tied to the tragic, linked to the lonely losers, and one with the weary wanderers? *Because that's who you are…you are one of them.*

The woman took my hand in hers tenderly. "Why…you cry?" she asked. "Your head…hurt too?"

Ted W. Mills was buried with no pomp or circumstance in the tiny Mills Family Cemetery on Uncle Jimmy's property in Egeria, WV. Only six human beings stood by the grave in silence. Out of the billions of beings on planet Earth, only *six* – not counting Tessa, who lay unconscious in a hospital in Amarillo – realized what the world had lost.

Tessa had a leg broken in two places, three cracked ribs, a concussion, and assorted deep bruises and lacerations. She was also in a coma for more than a week, and just when the doctors were doubting she'd ever come out of it, she did. A tear trickled from the corner of her eye as she suddenly smiled up at me. With a raspy, barely audible voice, she said, "You saved me." And then tears trickled from my eyes as well.

I stayed with Tessa at the hospital in Amarillo as much as I possibly could, leaving only when absolutely necessary to deal with the authorities regarding the crash of the Green Machine, and to help handle Ted's affairs and burial.

Tessa's pride didn't like it, but she needed someone to care for her for a while after she was released from the hospital. She would require several weeks of recuperation, at the very least. Uncle Jimmy insisted she stay with him, and after a modest display of protest, Tessa agreed. She really had nowhere else to go. Her parents passed away when she was a teenager, and she had only a handful of other relatives, most of whom she wouldn't have known if she passed them on the street.

As for me, I set out on foot for red rock country.

July 22, 1978

The tiny No Dinner Diner in Tucumcari, New Mexico, was filled with chattering customers, but the chattering stopped when I arrived in all my ragged glory. They turned to gaze at me as I stumbled inside. The place was thick with the sights and smells of scrambled eggs, country ham, hash browns, biscuits, gravy, orange juice and coffee. It was almost more than I could bear, and caused a gnawing in my stomach and a dizziness in my head.

The restaurant's slogan – "Eat Breakfast Like A King, Lunch Like A Prince, and Dinner Like A Pauper" – was prominently displayed, and in my ravenous state, I aspired to culinary royalty. I took an empty stool at the counter.

The man beside me tipped his hat back on his head and said, "Son, I git the feelin' you've had a streak of bad luck. From the looks of ya, I'd say ya busted a shit-load of mirrors."

"Yeah, bad luck," I said.

"Just passin' through, are ya?"

No, me and the wife and kids are thinking of settling down here. "Yes, I'm going to Arizona," I answered.

"Well, I'm 'a headin' that way soon as I have some grub. Tell ya what, I can give ya a ride, if ya want."

"Thank you," I said. "I don't have much, but I can pay you something for your trouble."

"Ain't necessary. Like I said, I'm goin' that way anyways." He stuck out a big, thick hand and said, "My name's Curt, Curt Conroy."

Curt Conroy was a large-boned, clean-shaven man with a wide, pink-skinned, friendly face, and silver hair beneath the brim of a white cowboy hat. He wore Lucchese Black Cherry cowboy boots, wrangler jeans, and a crisp denim shirt with western yokes. He chatted gregariously and at length with the waitress before placing his order, "Honey pot, give me a slab 'a fried ham, biscuits and gravy, hash browns, and Adam and Eve on a raft, and keep their eyes open."

The man never stopped talking. He talked while we waited for our food to arrive and he talked while we ate it, rarely pausing for me to get a word in, not that I particularly wanted to.

"I grew up in Rotan, Texas," he said. "Got my first job at Shorty's Service Station, then I was a roustabout in the oil fields at Hamlin, and then I ended up back in Rotan workin' at the Gypsum Plant. You ever been to Rotan? Prob'ly not. Not many folks have. Anyways, my daddy worked that plant for twenty-five years and he helped get me on. But I got restless and decided I'd try my hand as a petroleum engineer. Graduated from UT and got a job with Halliburton for a couple years. 'Course, the time I spent as a roustabout helped me a good bunch, ya know, havin' been out in the field."

The trucker rambled on and I nodded when appropriate, trying to conceal my congealing impatience. He seemed intent on recounting every step along his life's journey that had led him to that very moment at that very counter in that very diner on that very day.

My mind drifted... I saw myself slip and slide down a treacherous slope a heartache wide, toward three caskets side by side, occupied by three who died, by my hand or on my watch, a truth that could not be denied.

"You're probably wondering why I quit Halliburton." – *actually, no, I'm not* – "Well, truth is, it just wasn't for me. I like drivin' a truck and bein' my own boss on my own schedule. So I drive a rig, mostly haulin' oil field supplies across Texas and Oklahoma. Maybe it ain't quite as stable in some ways...Lord knows, especially these days, but, I manage to get by, and leastways, I'm my own man at the end of the day. This way I get the biscuit *and* the gravy. What more could a man want?"

I want you to shut up.

He laid payment on the counter with a big tip for the waitress, "Thank ya, honey pot. See ya next time 'round," he shouted her direction, and to me he said, "Come on, I'll show you my baby and we'll scoot on down the highway."

Curt Conroy's baby was a bright lemon-yellow Western Flyer Express 18-wheeler with a spacious cabin he called the lobby, and a large living-sleeping area he called home.

"Now, let's talk straight up front before we move one inch, just so we got an understanding. I'm a pretty a fair judge of a man's character and I got a feelin' you're an honest fella who's down on his luck. That's why I extended the offer. You're as welcome to ride with me as sunshine on a monsoon moon...but if you get the idea to try any kinda funny business, be forewarned that I'll have to bring forth my dispute-resolver."

With that, he deftly slid an old-fashioned Colt 9-shot pistol from a hidden holster on the left side of the driver's seat. "And I got a thirty-ought six-BAR behind the seat too," he added.

He drove leisurely – I'd expected as much – and had it not been for his non-stop narrative, I might have slept under the spell of the engine's steady moan, the sun's warm touch, and the never-changing landscape. Cows looked up with bemused interest – mouths working, tails swishing – as we passed by, and as Curt Conroy droned on, delivering a discourse on his life as a trucker. *Lucky cows.*

My mind did a cataclysmic tumble into twilight as I stared into the massive maze of switches, buttons, wires, digital readouts, compartments, communications center, and the gargantuan grid of gauges that filled the monstrous cabin. I saw the full floating faces of my fallen friends in the dials on the dash. Blood oozed from their mouths, nostrils, eyes and ears and gathered in the gully of guilt into which I'd fallen. I had memory stains on my brain, pain like rain down the drain and against the grain of my youthful, wishful thinking. There are happy endings on television, but rarely in real life.

Confined in the semi's lemon-colored cab, I leaned my head against the window and watched the receding road in the two angled side mirrors, each offering a slightly different perspective on the same thing – something that was gone.

Unfortunately, there are some 'gone' things that one can never truly escape, seismic searings that are permanently scorched into memory. Emily was one such scorching – she had been the epitome of erotica and the sovereign of sensuality – and my mind turned to her for some degree of comfort and distraction. *I wish to God she was alive and I could make love to her one more time, just be with her one last time before it's all over.* I closed my weary eyes to see her as Curt Conroy drove and droned on.

"We're travelin' holler, ya know…that's why we're makin'good time," Curt continued, "Done dropped my load in Louisiana. It was a rack of four and a half inch casin' for some small outfit doin' some drillin' over that way.

The radio was tuned to a Christian station with a country preacher hyperventilating over the Gospel of

198

Jesus Christ and babbling along beneath Curt's constant one-sided conversation. Mr. Conroy suddenly stopped talking, turned up the volume and listened closely to the minister's rant.

"I like to hear good preachers, them that gits fired up about their preachin'. If a man cain't git fired up 'bout what he believes, then he's no damn good at all. Now I ain't sayin' I agree with everythin' they say and I sure don't practice it all like a dee-vout Christian ort to, but I got things straight between me and the Big Man Upstairs, don't you think I don't, 'cause I surely do."

The Big Man Upstairs, I thought, smiling madly out the window. *Like the crazy uncle you lock in the attic.*

"I'll tell ya what I hate more'n anything," Curt continued. "Hypocrites. Ain't nothin' worse than a goddamn hypocrite. I don't claim to be no Christian, but by damn, if'n I did, I'd sure as hell toe the line. Got no patience for them that talk it but don't walk it."

He must not be Baptist.

We passed jack rabbits, diamond-backs, rusty 1964 F-100's, and a tent city in a gully where a hundred homeless, jobless, hopeless transients milled about with nowhere to go but the dirt.

"Damn, them poor folks has got it bad," Curt said. "But I guess plenty a' people do nowadays. If we had us a few damn leaders in Washington, maybe things woulda' been different…'Course, if we had some eggs, we could have ham and eggs, if we had some ham."

We came up quickly on a rusty brown pickup with a mattress and box springs strapped haphazardly to the back. The rope bindings were frayed and ratty, and the bedding hung limply over the sides and the roof of the cab. Curt bellowed at them with fist in air as he passed, "Damn fools! Beddin' should orta' be transported in an interior environment! I orta' run them fellas off the road."

"Why is that?" I asked.

"Cause my momma was killed by beddin'."

Puzzled, I stroked my bare chin where the hair, now folded in my pocket, had once been.

"I swear it's the truth, my hand to the Bible," Curt continued, his right hand raised in the air in the swearing position, "Momma worked the late shift at K-Mart. Comin' home one night, some folks had a mattress on top of their truck, just like that fella we just passed, and the wind caught it just right and lifted it up and off'n their truck. It come smack down on momma's windshield. She lost control, ran off the road, and hit one 'a them billboard signs for Cracker Barrel. She died on the spot, an angel gone to heaven."

The Caterpillar 600 engine groaned and the eighteen Michelins moaned as Curt Conroy wiped at his eyes with the back of his meaty hand. "A goddamn Cracker Barrel sign," he said despondently.

A goddamn Cracker Barrel sign.

"Ya know, I ain't never ate at one of their restaurants since, and God as my witness, I never will."

Anger and grief, like water on a hill, have got to go somewhere.

200

Albuquerque. I thanked Curt Conroy for the ride, and watched his yellow semi disappear into traffic. It was time to face the music, the discordant cacophony I'd fearfully and foolishly avoided ever since the crash. A bare-souled bearer of bad news, I knocked on my father's door.

He knew instantly that something was wrong. "What is it, son?"

I came straight out with it because I knew that was how my father liked things. "Ted's dead." Pause. "The Green Machine is totaled."

My father put a hand on my shoulder. It was the only time I could ever remember him touching me, other than to whip me. He whispered, "Damn. I'm sorry, son. Come on in the house."

Nothing was really resolved between my father and me, but some of the walls that separated us dissolved somehow. Perhaps it was simply the natural erosion that Time causes, or the impact of Death on those left behind, or Wisdom born of too much sorrow. All I know is that something changed.

My father and I spent a couple of days reminiscing about Ted, laughing at some of his foolish exploits, the weird way he talked – after the manner of the eccentric actor, Vincent Price – and his odd insistence on driving beat-up, old cars like the Studebaker. Our visit was low-key, reserved, and not overly weepy. We drank a few beers, ate some bologna sandwiches, and watched game shows on television. And then it was time for me to move on. Because I had a plan.

I'd never hugged my father before, but I thought it was high time I tried it. And though it was an awkward embrace, I didn't regret a second of it. Then, that night while he slept, I slipped away on foot – I wasn't about to ask him to borrow another vehicle – and pressed on toward Arizona to find a dark-skinned man named Omo.

Sedona

July 28, 1978

Six hundred and fifty miles after leaving Amarillo, having walked and hitched my way from state to state, I was in the land of red rocks and red dirt, an other-worldly landscape of beauty and mystery. Tired, wired, sweaty and hungry, I sat down in a restaurant called The Question Mark, which was not exactly the sort of name that inspired confidence in their dining fare. But I ordered anyway and was quickly drawn into an intriguing conversation underway in the booth next to mine.

"Prosperity is exactly what's *wrong*," a man in a dark brown Stetson was saying forcefully. "It knocked us clean off our foundation."

"You got about as much sense as a sprig of centipede grass," a man with wire rim glasses said. "You can't blame a man's problems on his possessions. It's his attitude toward them and what he does with them that matters."

"I'm not arguing that…I understand that. What I'm saying is…that excessive prosperity over a period of generations weakens a nation. It's just that simple, and I don't see how anyone could argue the point."

"How are we weak? I know things are really tough right now economically, and sure, we got plenty of problems--"

"Caused by too much prosperity!" the hat man interjected loudly, smacking his hand on the table.

"Will you let me finish my point?" The optically-challenged man threw up his hands in exasperation.

A matriarchal, white-haired woman seemed amused as she sipped her coffee. "Booker never was much on listening," she said, smiling at the man in the big hat, Booker, apparently. "He believes there are two sides to every issue – his side and the wrong side."

"Well, like I was trying to say," the man in glasses continued. "Things might be tough economically, but that doesn't make us weak, at least not in the sense you're talking about. We still have the most powerful and secure nation on the planet. Our military has technology so advanced that we could easily destroy any enemy, if we chose to do so. Now how can you call that weak?"

"Oh sure," Booker replied. "We have technology out the ass, but we have no inner fortitude. All the technology in the world won't matter when somebody pulls the plug on the electrical grid. Down in the trenches of warfare, or of life itself, what matters is resilience and fortitude - qualities we no longer possess."

"Don't you believe that mankind is continually evolving and becoming better as a species?" the woman asked softly.

"No, no, no, Havalka," Booker said. "Don't go down that path and try to change the subject. Stay on topic."

"But that *is* the same subject…or can't you see that?"

"What I'm trying to tell Harper, here," Booker continued. "Is that this country was built by pioneers with a bootstrap mentality. They overcame their enemies, the elements, the wilderness, and the cruel hand of fate. They had more backbone in their little finger than most people today have in their whole body. And that's because our prodigious prosperity has made us weak, short-sighted, self-absorbed, decadent, and opulent. And now we've raised up pampered generations of fat little children with fat little pets stuffing their fat little mouths with Twizzlers, French fries, corn dogs, pizza rolls, chocolate bars, and diet sodas. We're a nation born of too much, too fast, too soon, in a humanistic realm populated by hedonistic rubber-neckers and fatted calves juxtaposed against starving, homeless war veterans and anorexic, superficial supermodels."

Booker leaned way back in his seat and took a deep breath, his energy spent on his dynamic diatribe. Harper, the man in glasses, laughed raucously. "Good God Almighty, how long have you been practicing that speech?" he said. "I should call your wife right now and ask her how long you stood in front of the mirror working on that one."

"So," Havalka said, addressing Booker, "Let me see if I've got this straight. You don't believe that humanity is moving forward and evolving as a species. You think we're regressing, in spite of the overwhelming deluge of advancements in every field known to man. Sounds to me like you're focusing only on the negatives. Booker, you'd look at a thousand acres of prime pasture land and only see the cow patties."

"I'm talking about western civilization in general, the United States in particular. We are headed for a fall, my friends, a major fall, and folks had better take it seriously. We should be less like Nero and more like Machiavelli."

"Can't you imagine other possible scenarios?" Havalka continued. "Don't you believe in the innate goodness of man and our ability to reach a higher state of consciousness, one in which we will overcome our need to fight, conquer, possess and kill?"

I'd quickly and quietly ordered and eaten my meal during their discussion, but I could keep silent no longer. I turned in my seat and politely stepped into their conversation. "Men are brutes, born to fight to the bitter end, and nothing will ever change that. Nothing."

The three of them, along with a half dozen others who'd entered the restaurant after me, turned to gaze my way.

"Well, young man," Havalka said, "Your philosophy, and Booker's apparently, leave little room for the loftier ideals of faith, hope and love."

"Love may well be a powerful ingredient in society's stew," I said, preparing to leave. "But, in the end, it will not rise to the top, it will not conquer all. Death will always be the last one standing."

"So, then, what's the point of anything? According to you, we're nothing more than doomed sheep being led to the slaughter."

"Exactly."

"Hmmf," she snorted, and took a sip of coffee. "Well, I thank God that, unlike you, some people are still Pollyanna enough to believe that real change is possible, and that we'll find solutions to our problems and make the world a better place."

"I'm not so sure," I said softly. "Sometimes I wonder if we'd do just as well to put our faith in those cow patties you mentioned."

August 5, 1978

I rented a bedroom in a rundown house on the outskirts of Sedona from an equally rundown old Indian named Two Arrows. When I asked him how he got that name, he replied, "Because two arrows are better than one." And then he laughed like it was the world's funniest joke, laughed until a coughing fit kicked in. "Too much peyote," he said, clutching his side. "I'm trying to cut back, you know. My wife said smoking would be the death of me, but she died ten years ago, and I'm still here!" Then he started the laughing and hacking process all over again.

Zelma's Grocery Store gave me a blue apron, a box cutter, a pricing gun, a name tag, and a time card to punch. They told me to stack cases of vegetables on display beneath a sign that read "3 for 99 cents." And so I did – four rows of canned peas, four rows of canned corn, four rows of green beans, and four rows of every other vegetable that man has ever learned to can, each row aligned six cases high and three cases deep. That's a lot of vegetables.

They taught me to rotate my stock by pulling the old product to the front and putting the new in the back, a practice especially vital for perishable items like milk, eggs and produce. I also learned how to handle a pricing gun like a fast-draw gunslinger, and how to wield a box cutter like a swordsman, without slicing open a finger, arm or leg. Although, admittedly, I did learn have to learn that latter skill the hard and bloody way.

I kept a low profile in Sedona as I learned the ins and outs of my new part-time job as a grocery clerk in the great Southwest. It was a far cry from my whirlwind days as a guitar-slinging, rock & roll mini-god. And I was perfectly okay with that. I made casual friends and learned the rhythms and ways of the town; but remained on guard in the back of my mind, with an eye out for a shaved-head, dark-skinned devil.

Red Rock Riders gave me a flexible part-time job as a sort of jeep-driving chauffer and tour guide. So when I wasn't putting canned vegetables on grocery store shelves, I was studying the area's history and driving tourists through the ruggedly beautiful mountains and valleys in and around Sedona.

I met a lot of interesting people: game-cocks from South Carolina who were awed by Chicken Point, disco dancers who felt the old rhythms of Coyote Canyon, Christians who admired Devil's Tower, and atheists who worshipped at Cathedral Rock.

Sometimes Two Arrows rode with me on the tours, and provided a strong dose of authentic mysticism to complement the mesmerizing natural beauty of red rock country. The old Indian spoke of tribal shamans, Yavapai traditions, and myths and legends of the Sinaguan cliff dwellers. The customers loved it and before long, our tour was the most popular in town.

Often, as we took groups of tourists hiking near the Mogollon Rim, Two Arrows told stories of his ancestors. He kept his listeners spellbound with tales like the one about his great-grandfather, One Lung, who led his tribe to victory in a fierce battle against a horde of murderous invaders along the Red Rock of No Return.

"Why did they call him One Lung?" someone asked.

"Ah, that is a good question with another very good story," Two Arrows said. "When my great-grandfather was just a small boy, he came upon a fearsome grizzly bear. The beast slashed my great-grandfather across the chest, collapsing his left lung. But as the bear closed in to finish him off, my great-grandfather pulled his knife from its sheath and ran it through the bear's eye and into its brain, killing it instantly. My great-grandfather survived the terrible wound, became stronger for it, even though the lung never healed. From that day forth, they called him One Lung. And he lived to be 95 years old."

Later, back at the house, I asked Two Arrows, "Come on, was all that really true?"

"All what?"

You know...the bear...the one lung...that whole story."

The old Indian's face was creased with dark lines of age, and his eyes danced and sparkled like an imp. "Who can truly say what wonders are possible with the human body and spirit? You need more faith, young Brunky, more faith."

October 15, 1978

TWO Arrows didn't have a telephone, so whenever I could – which was several times a week – I'd borrow someone else's phone or use the one at Zelma's Store to call Tessa. She and I tried to cram as much conversation as possible into a few minutes, but there was never enough time.

"You should move out here with me," I'd always say at the end of the call.

"I would but Uncle Jimmy needs me here," she'd answer every time.

And in the background, I'd hear Uncle Jimmy say, "What the hell I need a damn girl hangin' around for? Go on, get your scrawny ass out to Arizona."

I could imagine the twinkle in his eye as he spoke, but it was the look in Tessa's eyes that I found myself really longing to see.

Uncle Jimmy mailed me several front page newspaper clippings – I did not let Two Arrows see them – from back home in West Virginia about me, Ted and Tessa. The articles explained how we'd been carjacked in Texas by a mysterious criminal who wrecked our vehicle and fled the scene, leaving the three of us for dead. They went on to describe how I, with superhuman strength, freed Tessa from the wreckage and carried her in my arms, on foot, 20 miles across the desert to safety. The articles painted me as some sort of larger-than-life, all-American hero.

But that wasn't how I saw it at all; I just did what anyone would have done. In *my* heart and mind, guilt and sorrow reigned supreme. I hadn't done enough to stop the madman, was too slow to act in the midst of the crisis, and shouldn't have allowed us to become victims in the first place. A guy like that isn't a hero; he's a failure. There was too much blood on my hands. I'd failed my mother, failed Emily, and finally, I failed my best friend. Some hero.

November 1, 1978

As the weeks and months passed, I created a new life in Sedona. But Emily and Ted were always with me, like ghosts wandering the wasteland of my mind, murmuring like un-avenged souls in limbo. My ultimate goal – to someday cross paths again with Omo – still simmered quietly on the back burner of my brain. The fact that the dark man had said he lived in red rock country was the only clue I had to go on, and was the initial driving force behind my relocation to the area.

So I continued to work my jobs, hang out with Two Arrows, mingle with the locals and tourists, and hope that somehow, somewhere, I'd see Omo again. When I had free time, I even scoured the county courthouses in the area hoping I might spot his unusual name in their records, maybe on a property deed, tax record or marriage license. The odds were ridiculously long – I knew that – but I decided to follow the old axiom: *You may not be in the right place at the right time, but you can go to the right place and wait.*

While living in Sedona, I attempted to keep my old life to myself, and suppress the nightmares that had haunted me for so long. I'm not sure how I accomplished it, but I kept my mother quiet for months. Perhaps my outpouring of grief and confession to Ted's corpse that day by the wreckage in Texas cleansed my soul. Or maybe it was simply my mother's doing. But the pessimistic part of me figured she'd be back eventually, standing front and center with her voice raised in condemnation. She always came back.

The mountains in red rock country are like the mountains of West Virginia in one unfortunate regard: they both get very cold in the winter.

I complained to Two Arrows, "This is the desert southwest…I thought it was always warm here."

"You thought wrong, paleface," Two Arrows joked with his trademark, crooked grin. "Just wait till January."

"You know, you're doing absolutely nothing to make me feel better. In fact, you seem to be enjoying my discomfort."

"Grow a beard," he continued. "It will help keep you warm. Besides, you look like a man who needs a beard."

"Yeah, I actually had a weird sort of goatee for years," I said. "The hair on my chin hung down to about here," – I put my hand at my sternum to illustrate before continuing – "and it became my trademark look. Sometimes I dyed it different colors."

"Why did you shave it off?"

I hesitated, not wanting to reveal anything more. "I just got tired of it," I said flatly.

Two Arrows didn't believe me but he let it slide. "I think it's time you grow it back."

And so I did.

"So, who is this Ted person?" Two Arrows asked.

I was startled by his question. "What? How do you know...what do you mean?"

"I eavesdropped on you when you were talking to your girlfriend on the store phone yesterday."

"Tessa? She's not my girlfriend."

"She sounds like your girlfriend."

"Well..." I hesitated for a long time. "She's not."

"You did not answer my question."

"You were eavesdropping on me?" I said indignantly.

Two Arrows grinned and his shook back his long silver hair. "How else you think I get to be so wise?"

I wasn't really angry with him, but I stormed out anyway. For effect.

January 3, 1979

"**So,** who is this Ted?" Two Arrows asked again over breakfast the next morning, as he poured a full cup of sugar on his Corn Flakes.

"Are you crazy?" I said. "All that sugar can't be good for you."

"Who says?"

"Uh, well, doctors, I guess," I replied.

"They don't even know how to cure the common cold. What do they know about sugar?"

I spread my hands apart and shrugged my shoulders.

"Life is full of things bitter and sour; why deny one's self the sweet? I say you can never have too much sugar," Two Arrows countered. "Now, who is Ted?"

I rolled my eyes. "You won't give up, will you?"

"Give up is for losers. Do I look like a loser?"

His hair was wilder that Medusa's, he had milk dribbling down his chin, and he was wearing a ratty, cotton robe that revealed far too much of his skinny legs.

I said, "Do you want me to answer that truthfully?"

"Who is Ted?" he repeated, crunching on cereal. "You might as well tell me or I will use the Spirit Power to pull it from your brain. And that can be most unpleasant."

I studied the old guy for a minute as he poured more sugar onto his flakes. I was a pretty sure he was harmless, and I doubted he could actually suck information from my mind, but I wasn't entirely convinced.

"Alright," I said with a long sigh. "Ted, Ted W. Mills, was my best friend in the world. We met in junior high school and became inseparable. He was closer than any brother could ever be…he was always there for me…always had my back…and there wasn't a truer soul on earth than Ted."

Two Arrows nodded solemnly as if he knew *exactly* what I was talking about. "Those such as your friend are rare, very rare. What happened to him?"

I bit on the inside of my cheek. "He died…in a car wreck…about six months ago."

"And then you moved here," Two Arrows said. "To start fresh."

"Yeah, that pretty much sums it up."

"And what about this Tessa?"

I hesitated for a long moment. "Well, she was Ted's girlfriend and my good friend."

Two Arrows held up his cereal bowl with both hands, tipped it up to his lips, and drank down the last of its sugary contents. With a milk moustache, he said, "The two of you share a great sorrow. You can comfort each other. Maybe she will come visit."

Tessa was standing at the screen door, silhouetted against the setting sun, peering in as Two Arrows and I drank beer and ate TV Dinners – even though we had no TV to watch.

"Knock, knock," Tessa called out. "Anybody home?"

I jumped up and ran to the door. "Tessa? Oh, my God! Tessa, is that you?"

"Of course it's me. Who else would it be?" she laughed. "Do you regularly have other young, beautiful women knocking on your door?"

"You're the only one," I said as I opened the door and took her in my arms. We embraced for a very long time in silence. I didn't know about her eyes but there were tears in mine.

Finally, Two Rivers cleared his throat. "You two should get a room."

The spell broken, Tessa and I ended our embrace and laughed nervously.

"Why didn't you tell me you were coming? What are you doing here?" I asked.

"I came to visit," Tessa said simply. "And I wanted to surprise you."

"Well, mission accomplished. It is so great to see you!" I said, turning toward Two Arrows. "Can she stay here with us? Is that alright?"

In his most serious tone, Two Rivers said, "Yes, but she must bed with me."

Tessa and I looked at the old Indian with uncertainty until he burst out in laughter. "You should have seen your pale faces!" He laughed until another of his coughing fits came on.

"Did Brunky tell you about how he saved my life?" Tessa asked.

Two Rivers gave me a disapproving, fatherly look. "No, he said nothing at all about such a thing. He spoke of you endlessly day and night, but mentioned nothing about the saving of a life."

Then it was Tessa's turn to give me a look. "How could you not tell him about that? You're way too modest."

I took Tessa's arm and gently steered her toward the kitchen as she protested, "What are you doing? What's wrong with you?

"Please excuse us for a moment, Two Arrows," I said.

"I do not like secrets," Two Arrows called after us.

I leaned in close to Tessa and whispered, "Since I've been here, I've just tried to keep my past private as much as possible, especially, you know…the wreck…the details of all that."

"But why?" Tessa asked.

"Because I spent so much time wallowing…in a funk…just like Ted said. He was right."

"Yes, but there's a big difference between wallowing and simply stating the truth about things that happened," Tessa argued. "The fact is: you saved my life and you're a hero."

"Oh, come on," I said. "Please don't start with that hero crap."

Tessa shook her head and rolled her eyes at me.

"See, this is exactly the kind of conversation I don't want to get into," I said. "If I go back down this road, before I know it, the dreams will come back, the darkness will take hold of me, and my mother's damn voice will be yammering in my head again."

Tessa embraced me warmly and whispered, "Okay, okay. We'll just let it be for now."

It felt good to be held.

Tessa and I hiked and climbed to the Vortex and sat on Kachina Woman. The great rock formation was inundated with tourists soaking in the beauty, mediums channeling the various tongues of God, and mystics balancing their chakras with the cosmic waves reverberating from the stone.

"See that scraggly plant over there?" Tessa asked, pointing. "It reminds me of the burning bush in the Bible."

"How do you know what the burning bush looked like?" I asked.

"I did a lot of reading while I was laid up," she said with a smile. "The actual plant in the third chapter of Exodus was *Rubus Sanctus*, or at least, that's what Jewish tradition says. It's a sort of bramble bush that burned with fire but wasn't consumed by it. And that's where God spoke to Moses to give him--"

"Wow, you really *did* do a lot of reading."

"A lot of thinking, too," Tessa added.

Later, when we arrived back at the house, we found Two Arrows in a trance-like state, sitting cross-legged in the floor, surrounded by crystals, feathers and assorted Indian artifacts. The smell of marijuana was thick in the air. Tessa and I tried to tiptoe by so as not to disturb him.

"Welcome home," Two Arrows said softly.

"Sorry, we were trying not to intrude upon your prayers or meditation...or whatever it is you're doing," I said.

"The return of friends is never a disturbance. Sit with me and tell me about your day."

And so we sat.

"We had great time," Tessa said. "We went to the Vortex and I could feel the vibrations of the rock moving through me."

"Yes, yes," Two Arrows said. "And you marveled at the Burning Bush."

Tessa and I looked at each other with surprise, and then at the old Indian.

"How did you...how could you know that?" Tessa asked, wide-eyed.

"Did you follow us?" I said accusingly.

"I most certainly did not," Two Arrows said. "I am the Vortex, as are you."

February 14, 1979

Tessa and I were sitting on the small porch with our feet propped up on the wooden banister, watching the sun play on the red cliffs and towering spires. Shadows shifted in the rock like phantoms and the cloudless sky blazed what I was certain must have been a previously unknown hue of blue.

"My God," Tessa said. "It's so very, very beautiful here. I've never seen….or *felt* anything like this place."

"I know exactly what you mean. There's something very healing here that resonates within me, almost like it's calling me. The longer I've been here, the more I've felt it."

Tessa studied me closely.

Slightly embarrassed, I said, "I know, I know, you think I'm a little crazy."

"Oh, I already knew you were crazy," Tessa said. "But that's not what I was thinking. I was thinking about how much I missed you."

"Yeah, me too," I said.

"Hard to believe you're the same ragged guy I met that day in the hotel when Ted and I rescued you. Lord, you were a mess."

"Yeah," I said softly. "I surely was…"

There was another long silence as the sun shifted into a more comfortable position a little lower in the sky.

"These last two weeks here have been so great," Tessa said.

I nodded. "I couldn't agree more."

227

"So," Tessa said, drawing the syllable out.

"So what?" I said cautiously.

"Well, I was just thinking…I don't want to overstay my welcome…" her voice trailed off.

"Impossible."

"I really do feel bad about taking your bed and making you sleep on the couch. Why don't we switch? At least I'd feel a little less guilty."

"Not necessary," I said.

She lowered her voice and leaned closer to me. "What about Two Arrows? You think he's getting sick of me hanging around? I mean, this is his house, right?"

I was about to answer her when the old Indian stepped out on the porch and let the screen door bang behind him, startling us immensely.

"You're always sneaking up on people," I said. "Could you stop that?"

Two Arrows ignored me and said, "Young lady, don't you know that Indians can hear *very* well? If you're wondering whether I've grown tired of your company, you should just ask me directly."

Tessa's face was flushed. I'd never seen her embarrassed before. "Well, Mr. Arrows, I, uh…"

Two Arrows smiled and ended her misery. "Of course you can stay here as long as you wish. Brunky is poor company but you are most enjoyable. Therefore, it balances out. And as you know, Indians believe in harmony and balance in all things."

"Thank you so much," Tessa said as she jumped up and flung her arms around the Indian's neck.

"Happy Valentines Day," Two Arrows said.

228

The days passed quickly with Tessa in Sedona. I worked my part-time shifts at the grocery store, and ran jeep tours through the back country three days a week. In the evenings, Tessa and I watched the sunset in all its southwestern glory, while Two Arrows cooked up some outrageous native American dish of rattlesnake, gopher, squirrel or, worst of all, some disgusting concoction he called hominy stew.

For a while, there was a sense of normalcy and peace about my life, and some days, it was hard for me to imagine that I was the same guy, that tortured soul, who had been driven to the edge of insanity only eight months before. I couldn't help wondering…once you've teetered on that ledge and stared into the horrifying abyss, can you ever truly recover? It was frightening to think of how easily I could have turned out like Emily, fallen prey to so many terrible demons and addictions.

As for my self-appointed task…yes, I still wanted to find Omo, still wanted revenge, and those things continued to lurk in the back of my mind. But did I *really* think I'd ever find Omo? Honestly, no, I did not. And so I took one day at a time, and did my best to build a new life and escape the bitter man I used to be.

"Come on, get up, I want to take you somewhere," I said, pinching Tessa's toe as she lay sprawled on the sofa.

"Where?" Tessa asked without looking up, her head buried in a book about the Yavapai culture and history.

"We're going out," I said firmly. "I want to show you something cool."

Tessa jumped up with a mischievous grin. "You're taking me out? Oh, is this a date? Should I put on something nice?"

"Oh, shut up," I said playfully.

"Now, mister man, that is no way to talk to your date."

"This isn't a date. Look, do you want to go or not?"

She giggled and said, "Give me just a minute and I'll be ready."

As we went out the door, we met Two Arrows returning home from the market with a paper bag full of groceries in each arm. "Ah," he said with great pleasure. "I see you two are going out on a date. Good for you!"

I started to speak but held my tongue. *How does he do that?* Slightly embarrassed by the entire situation, I jumped into the Jeep without a word while they just stood there grinning at each other.

"Are you coming or not?" I said.

Tessa just raised her eyebrows at Two Arrows and shrugged. "Coming, love." Then she kissed the old Indian on the cheek and climbed in beside me.

We swung by The Cowboy Club and got buffalo burgers and cactus fries to go. Then, crossing creek beds and leaning low beneath the arms of twisted juniper trees, we followed a rugged trail to Submarine Rock. There we climbed to the top to dine, and take in the 360 degree, full-scale view of the entire region. We could see for miles and miles in every direction, and I pointed out a few of the landmarks I'd learned so far – Munds Mountain, Marg's Draw, Wilson Mountain, and the town of Sedona itself.

Tessa gasped with joy. "Wow, it makes my head spin. Just when you think you've seen everything…" her voice trailed off, and she turned to look at me. It wasn't just your normal look; it was one that lasted a good long time, and carried with it a powerful significance. She stared into my eyes, and I stared back. I wasn't sure if I was still breathing or if I'd gone on to meet my Maker. I couldn't determine what was on her mind, but I distinctly remember thinking *Uh, oh.*

Finally, she whispered, "Thank you," locked her arm in mine and put her head on my shoulder.

Red Rock Riders sent me to pick up two customers who were renting me and the Jeep for at least a couple of days. I was expected to be at their beck and call, and I agreed to the deal because the boss assured me that the money would be *very* good. So, as instructed, I drove north to Flagstaff and stood outside the small terminal, holding up a placard that read: *Ferguson.*

I saw the woman first. She was stunning. Her hair was golden like the sun on a summer day, and her skin was the color of wheat, freshly threshed. She wore a whisper-white dress, dangling turquoise earrings, and a twisted hemp sash. She extended her hand and said, "Hello, my name is Opal Ferguson. You must be our driver."

My tongue actually got twisted around in my mouth and I felt like a complete idiot. I swallowed hard and said, "Yes...yes...I am that...your driver, that is."

She smiled and turned away to scour the crowd for her companion. "Oh, here he comes," she said with an odd tone to her voice. It was almost as though a bitter jigger of fear had been poured into her glass of anticipation.

I followed her gaze and there he was – a muscular, black man who was probably eight inches taller than me and outweighed me by a hundred pounds. He had a shaved head and a smile that was one part vile vulture and one part cold-hearted reptile.

Omo.

In the flesh and much bigger than I remembered.

The hair on my arms and on the back of my neck stood up and tried to scream.

Wearing my croc hat and sunglasses, and with my goatee grown back, I was reasonably sure he didn't recognize me from that one fateful evening nearly a year ago. Truth is, he barely seemed to notice me at all. I suppose I was just another minion to him.

We went south on Route 89 in silence, but ten miles outside of Sedona, Omo said, "Take this trail to the right."

And so I did. *At your beck and call, asshole.*

We drove 20 miles into the barren wilderness, into an area with which I was completely unfamiliar. I stole occasional glances at Omo and Opal in my rearview mirror, hoping they'd give me some indication of where we were going. As always, I had emergency supplies and my guns with me, but I was still beginning to get a little nervous.

Finally, I asked, "So, where are we headed?" trying to sound as nonchalant as possible.

"We are headed for grand adventure," Omo said.

That made me uncomfortable. Those were almost the exact words he'd spoken that night on the north Texas plains.

Probably sensing my unease, Opal spoke up, "We are headed for a small cantina."

"A cantina? Out here? You must be kidding."

"There is much you do not know," Omo said. "Just drive."

"We're almost there," Opal said. "Just a few more minutes."

She was right. We topped a rise and there below us was an oasis of sorts – four small buildings partially obscured by a thick stand of lush, well-tended trees and bushes. I saw a four-wheeler, a few bikes, and maybe a half dozen people moving about the area. I pulled in front of the tiny cantina and Omo and Opal went inside.

In a moment, Opal returned and took me by the hand. "I won't have you sitting out here alone; I insist that you join us for a drink. You look like you could use one."

"No, no, I'd probably best wait here," I said.

I desperately needed time to gather my wits about me, make a plan. I'd held myself together while in their presence, but once they'd gone inside the café, I began shaking and sweating as the gravity of the situation hit me hard. Even though I'd been seeking Omo for so long, his sudden appearance had still taken me off-guard. It's true what they say about life: things happen when you least expect them.

"You must come in. I won't take no for an answer," Opal insisted, tugging on my arm. "You've driven a long way and it's very hot out here. Come sit inside with us beneath the fan and have a cold drink."

I relented, took a deep breath, followed Opal inside, and sat down with her at their table. Omo was in a back corner, speaking in hushed tones with two mysterious characters. One of them was dressed in a white suit and hat, while the other wore fatigues and had at least a hundred tattoos on his body. I watched them closely and spotted a speedy and surreptitious exchange: a package for an envelope. Omo looked inside the envelope, seemed satisfied with what he saw, and slid it quickly into his pocket.

I looked away and turned my eyes back to Opal at the table. Grinning madly, she whispered with a bit of a slur in her voice, "He is a dealer."

"What do you mean?" I asked.

She put her fingers clumsily to her lips in the universal shushing motion, and giggled like a little girl, which she most certainly was not.

Is she drunk? I wondered

Suddenly Omo was back at the table. To a man in a corner he shouted, "Music!" and the man began to play a battered, slightly out-of-tune upright piano.

"Dance, woman," Omo commanded Opal loudly. "Dance for me."

She stood quickly and struck a pose. Blue and green exploded in her eyes like the water in Prudhoe Bay, and she flung herself into the music the way that great chunks of glacier plunge into the Arctic Sea. She held her sandals in her hand and stirred up wisps of dust with her bare feet as she danced to rhythms I desperately wanted to share, but could not.

Transfixed, Omo watched the woman dance across the veranda and out into the clearing where lush plants thrust their leafy stalks into the warm, late afternoon air. And I watched Omo watching her. His skin was dark brown as the richest loam of the Fertile Crescent. His countenance was smooth and calm, yet something unnerving seethed beneath the surface. His lips curled into an expression that combined beguiling grin with treacherous smile, to form something that I supposed could have been called a grile.

In our cups was an eerie elixir that seemed to go to my head almost before I swallowed. *Maybe this is what Opal drank and the reason she's suddenly behaving so strangely.*

Opal returned to our table, peered into her drink and said, "I see bits of fingers, frog's blood, and oxen stool. I want to go somewhere else."

"Of course," said the dark man with the grile. "I know another place."

"I suspected you would," Opal said as she lay her head down on the table and laughed. Unlike Omo, there was no guile to her smile. She rolled her head from side to side, slowly, causing her long blonde tresses to stroll and tumble in bits and bunches about her face. Between strands, she peered out at us, and at the world, like a child playing peekaboo.

As we left the café, the day was waning like that sad, certain moment when the bright buzz of the bee becomes a weary drone. As we climbed into the topless Red Rider Jeep, it occurred to me that, after all this time waiting to find Omo, I had no plan of action. Nothing. Zilch. All I could do was drive and see how things played out.

My two traveling companions wedged themselves into the tiny back seat, and I adjusted the rear-view mirror slightly to be able to watch them as I drove. They paid no heed to me, except once…once when the woman locked eyes with me in the mirror and smiled like a knowing cat.

Omo caressed her smooth inner thighs and she spread them. He reached in further and flipped her purring switch to the ON position. She cupped his ebony face in her small hands and began to kiss him, nipping at him at first like a hummingbird in honeysuckle. Then, plunging full in, she made love to his mouth with hers.

It was difficult to keep my eyes on the road ahead with what was happening in the seat behind me.

Omo lifted Opal and pushed her down upon his exposed hardness. The woman cried out in pain. "Too big, too big," she mumbled over and over, as he forced her up and down, up and down. Then suddenly, Omo pushed her off him, and grabbed her viciously by her blonde locks. "Open your mouth and taste the nectar of the Gods!" he shouted. "Swallow the seed of your master."

The ranch house was hidden at the back end of a small canyon a few miles from the cantina, and I dropped my two passengers there at one o'clock in the morning. I was more than happy to be free of them, even if only for a few hours. I needed to get my head on straight and formulate a plan. *Good luck with that.*

High on adrenaline, low on sleep and in the middle of a precarious situation, I rushed home to tell Tessa what had happened. She did not take the news well.

"Tessa, Tessa, wake up," I said, shaking her from sleep.

"What…what is it?" she mumbled, rubbing her eyes. "What's wrong?"

"I found him. He's here in Sedona," I said.

Tessa sat up in the bed, looking puzzled. "What? Who are you talk--" And then it hit her. "Omo?! Oh, my God! He's actually here?"

"Yes. He and a woman friend are staying at a place way outside of town."

"I can't…I just can't hardly believe it," she said. "Are you sure it's him?"

I gave her a look.

She jumped out of bed and paced, her mind racing, her mouth running in whisper mode so as not to disturb Two Arrows. "How did you find him? What happened? Did you talk to him? We should call the police, right? Wow, my brain is going a mile a minute. I just can't believe this…"

In the moonlight streaming through the window, I couldn't help noticing that Tessa was wearing only a black bra and panties. Focused intently on the situation at hand, she was oblivious to what she was or was not wearing. I, however, was fully aware.

She stopped suddenly and turned to me. "What are you planning to do, Brunky? Please tell me you're not thinking something crazy."

"You know what you're going to do," an eerie voice said from the doorway behind us. It was Two Arrows.

"Damn, you scared the snot out of me," Tessa said.

The Indian ignored her. Instead, his gaze remained steady, burning a hole through me.

"How do you know what I'm going to do?" I asked. "How do you even know anything about this?"

"You came here on a vision quest of sorts," Two Arrows said. "Isn't this true?"

I was suddenly shaking again.

Two Arrows pressed on. "Is it redemption you want? Or is it revenge?"

"Can I have both?" I asked.

"Maybe."

"Listen, guys," Tessa interrupted. "I think we should just get to a phone and call the police."

"No," I said firmly.

"When a snake is at your feet, you do not call the police," Two Arrows said.

Tessa and I looked at the old man with bewilderment.

"Look down," he said.

We did. There was a large, rattling serpent at our feet.

"Snake!" I yelled, my voice at least an octave higher than normal.

"Snake!" Tessa harmonized with a heady mix of adrenaline and fear.

238

"Snake!" I repeated as if redundancy might charm the reptile.

She and I tangled with each other as we tried to jump up on the bed. Snakes had always made me very nervous, and I pictured the killer clamping down on my leg, shooting its poison through my body, and rendering me helpless as it dragged me back to its lair where it would feast upon my flesh.

But the snake did not pursue us; it merely rattled its tail in the center of the room as if trying to decide whom to bite first.

As these events unfolded, Two Arrows took a pinch of something from a pouch on his belt, put it in his mouth and chewed it quickly, but did not swallow. Then, in a flash, he stepped on the snake and grabbed it at the base of its head so that it could not bite. Holding it up only inches from his face, he stared into the snake's eyes as it writhed about wildly and wrapped around his arm.

"What the hell are you doing?" I shouted.

"Get it out of here!" Tessa said.

Instead, Two Arrows spit in the snake's face, coating its entire head with a nasty, sticky mass of brown sludge.

"Eewww, gross," Tessa said.

The serpent convulsed for a few moments and then went rigid, hard, and straight as a broomstick.

Tessa and I were shocked incredulous. "Okay, now, what the hell was *that*?" I said. "You just blew my mind."

"You should not be surprised. Doesn't your Good Book tell you that man shall have dominion over all the beasts of the field? Now, here," Two Arrows said, holding the snake-stick out toward me.

"Here *what*?" I said. "I don't want that."

"Take it with you and use it against your foe. Time is of the essence; now go face your destiny."

239

Tessa said, "Are you encouraging him to go fight Omo?"

"I do not even know who or what an Omo is," Two Arrows said. "I only know that Brunky must do that which has been placed in his heart. The foe's name is irrelevant; it differs for each of us. But the mission is the same for all people."

I couldn't believe I was doing it, but I reached out and took the stiff snake from the old Indian.

"No, no, no," Tessa pleaded with me. "You shouldn't do this."

"Omo is an evil man," I said. "He killed my best friend and nearly killed us too. Then he walked away like we were nothing."

"Brunky…" Tessa whispered, her voice trailing off.

"Tessa, I moved here for one reason only – to find that bastard and make him pay for what he did. And now he's been practically laid in my lap. I have to do what I have to do."

"And what is that, exactly?" Tessa asked.

I gave her a steely look of determination and answered, "I'm not sure yet."

"Well, that's great, just great," she said sarcastically.

But before she could say anything else, I kissed her full on the mouth, and ran from the house.

My jeep threw up a storm of dust and debris as I roared away from the house in the black of night. The last thing I heard was Tessa calling out, "Brunky, don't do this! Come back! Two Arrows, do something. Please stop him."

But there was no stopping me. I wasn't sure what I was doing, but I was doing it. I flew up Boynton Pass and out into the barren wilderness, worked my way around

Bear Mountain and along the base of Lost Mountain. I wound carefully along talus slopes, through a valley of conifer and aspens, and past stands of early-blooming penstemon, lupine and paintbrush that were glorious even in the moonlight.

Butted up against steep cliffs and rocky slopes, Omo's camp was shielded on three sides by red rock. Since coming straight up the driveway was definitely not an option, I parked the Jeep out of sight a half mile away and approached on foot in the moonlight.

Dawn was still at least an hour away as I climbed – using my reptilian walking stick – up a steep knoll spotted with boulders, brush and juniper trees. A dim light glowed in the front window of the house a hundred yards below me, and I watched the area for a while in silence, scanning through binoculars, though they weren't much help in the semi-darkness. A fire burned in an open pit out front and sent dark shadows dancing. Other than that, there was no sign of life; all the vehicles that had been there the night before were gone.

What now, Brainiac?

As I sat in the dirt contemplating, I checked the Remington to make sure it was loaded, and felt for my Beretta just to be double-sure it was still in my pocket. Of course, I didn't really plan to shoot the man. *Or did I?* I'd never shot anyone in my life. It just felt good knowing I was armed…just in case. *In case what?*

The night air was cold and I took a long drink from the flask in my jacket pocket. It warmed me up right away and steadied my nerves. So I had another. And another. *Nothing beats vodka in a crisis,* I laughed to myself.

At the gate of Omo's ranch house was an eight-foot high ceramic horse that stood reared up on its hind legs, the verisimilitude of a true wild steed from the old West, a

241

stationary stallion forever posed in helpless rebellion against captivity. As clouds danced across the face of the moon, it seemed as though the horse's eyes went wild with fear. I rubbed my eyes and looked again through my binoculars.

In my nine months in Sedona, I'd heard plenty of stories about paranormal activities, witchcraft, and aliens in the area's canyons, chasms and buttes. Places like Jerome and the Bradshaw Ranch were famous for ghost sightings, unexplained disappearances, and even little green – or gray, depending on whom you spoke to – men. From Thunder Mountain to Coyote Canyon – perhaps as a sort of polar opposite to the beauty and spirituality of the place – red rock country was ripe with ghastly stories of torture, ritualistic sacrifices, and assorted psychic phenomena. I'd found it all fascinating but not given it too much serious thought. Until now.

As I lay on my belly in the red dirt, the hair on my arms suddenly stood up as if with static electricity, and I felt as though I was being watched. I mustered my courage and looked around, expecting to see a coyote or a bear or Omo or goblins or something. But there was nothing but the pre-dawn gloom. So I took another swig from my bottle and thought about the situation.

Okay, I need a plan; I mean, what am I actually doing here? Am I going to fight Omo? Shoot him? Turn him in to the police, and have him charged for carjacking and killing Ted? What would that be – manslaughter?

I felt the chill of fear sweep over me yet again, and goose bumps popped up all over my body. Quietly, carefully, I shifted into a crouching position behind some brush, and kept my head on a slow swivel so that no one could get the jump on me. I saw no one and nothing.

At best, there's maybe an hour till sunrise; so, whatever I do, I need to do it soon. In the darkness, I

242

have an advantage because I know exactly where Omo is, but he has no clue where I am. For all he knows, I'm at home, asleep in my bed.

"I know you're there," a voice called out.

I froze, staring down toward the house in the gully. *That voice sounded familiar. Was it Omo? Where did it come from? Oh, my God, is he inside my freaking head?!*

And then a figure stepped from the shadows and into the firelight below. It was him. He bent casually toward the fire, lit a cigar and puffed it vigorously.

"Your time is short, my friend," he called out to the hills. Even from a football field away, I could see his curling, vicious, white-toothed smile through the binoculars as he turned and walked back inside the house.

Who was he talking to? Was that intended for me? How could he know I'm up here? That's impossible.

Faint murmuring rose up to me from the house. It almost sounded like…whimpering. *Odd.*

I listened and thought for a few more minutes, hoping a brilliant idea might reveal itself. But none came. And so finally I decided it was time to take action via the direct approach. I figured I'd simply go down there and confront my destiny. "The man's a son of a bitch, plain and simple," I said softly to myself. "It's time I face him for what he did to Ted…what he did to all of us."

Stealthily, snake-stick in one hand and Remington .45 in the other, I crept down the steep hillside and approached the house from the leeward direction where there was more ground cover. With only one window on that side, I crawled to it, stretched up on my tiptoes, and peeked in ever so carefully.

I saw Opal stretched out in the form of a human X, her arms and legs bound tightly to a steel frame bed that had no mattress. Her clothes were shredded, hanging loosely in tatters about her, and her near-naked body glistened with sweat and was dripping blood. I couldn't help thinking of one of my father's favorite sayings: *The cat's out of the bag...and it's a fucking lion.*

Omo moved around her, circling the bed casually, smiling like the cat that tortured, butchered, and ate the canary. Opal was gagged but she murmured, moaned, and swiveled her head from side to side. She seemed to be pleading with him.

My God, what is he doing to her?

I quickly studied the scene. There were at least a dozen wires attached to various parts of Opal's body, including her breasts and genitals; and those wires were connected to what appeared to be a generator. There was also a mechanical device of some sort – it looked like a drill with a large plastic or rubber bit – positioned between her legs.

Omo was speaking to her softly, almost cooing as he circled her; I could hear him vaguely, but couldn't make out the words. He turned a knob on the generator and it began to hum; Opal quivered and moaned. It suddenly dawned on me that Omo was sending an electric current through her body.

He flipped a switch on the drill and it pushed inward between Opal's legs. She groaned madly, and her eyes went crazy wild like a rabid animal. Then Omo increased the current from the generator, and Opal's body shuddered and lifted up from the bed like a possessed woman.

I moved quickly and quietly along the side of the house, stepped up carefully on the wooden porch, and found the front door ajar. *Strange.* I took a deep breath to try to steady my nerves, steeling myself for whatever was to come. It didn't seem to work; I could hear the blood pounding in my ears like sonic booms.

"Come in, Brunky," a voice said from somewhere in the shadows inside. *So much for the element of surprise.*

Leading with the pistol – just like I'd seen them do in cop shows – I started carefully through the opening. But Omo was behind the door, and he smashed it on my wrist, immediately knocking the gun from my hand. I yelled out in pain as he grabbed my arm, twisted it, and pulled me inside the house. He kicked the Remington across the room and underneath a table in the far corner.

"Well, dear boy, I am so pleased you stopped by," Omo grinned. "I assume you've come to join us for the festivities. Perhaps you would like a soft drink or some Hors d'oeuvres?"

I couldn't take my eyes off of Opal.

"Now, now, you must not worry about the lady," Omo said. "She likes it this way, rough. It's her 'thing,' you know. She is what you would call kinky."

Opal shook her head vigorously, crazily, from side to side, and tears poured from her eyes and rolled down her face. She made loud pleading sounds from within the gag stuffed deep in her mouth.

"She doesn't look like she's enjoying it," I said, trying to put up a front of cool confidence. "Let her go."

"Oh, now, Mr. Brunky, surely you would like to watch for a while? You seem like the kind of boy who likes to watch. I shall turn the machines back on for you so you can see how she enjoys it. You'd like that, wouldn't you?"

"You are one sick, demented bastard," I said as I moved boldly toward the bed.

"The tread on your boots will not suffice on this particular trail," Omo said. "You will lose your footing and take a most serious fall."

I ignored him and reached to undo the strap around Opal's wrist; thinking that maybe if I quickly untied her and we brazenly walked out, he might just let us go.

I was wrong.

Omo spun me around and shouted, "I invited you inside as a courteous gesture of hospitality, but that does not give you the right to interfere with how I run affairs in my home."

I summoned more false bravado and said, "Omo, keep pushing me and you will be sorry."

He laughed with utter disdain. "You are nothing more than a piss ant to me. I can crush you under my heel at any moment, just as I did your beloved, pathetic friends."

Hell-fire rage shot up my spine, and I swung at the big man with my snake walking-stick. Omo blocked the blow and wrestled the hardened snake away from me. Miraculously, the very moment he took possession of it, the reptile sprang back to life, wrapped around Omo's arm, and sank its fangs deep into his right bicep.

"Apache voodoo!" he shrieked with eyes wide as flying saucers. Omo swung his arm wildly and tried to pry the snake loose, but it clung ever more tightly to him. "I curse you and your children and your children's children," he screamed at me. "You will all burn!"

Suddenly, I remembered my Beretta and desperately tried to wrest it free from my pocket as we scuffled. But Omo reached for me clumsily with his left hand and caught me by the binocular strap around my neck. I attempted to break loose but he twisted the strip of leather around my neck, tighter and tighter until it was tearing into my skin, bringing blood and crushing my windpipe.

As I gagged and gasped for breath, Omo put his face to mine, nose to nose, and smiled that evil, condescending grile of his; even as the snake's venom pulsed through his body, and even as my life's breath ebbed from mine. He just kept smiling.

"I may die," he hissed. "But you die too."

I clawed at the band of leather around my neck, and screamed with rage but no sound came out.

"You are afraid to die! I see it in your eyes!" Omo roared. "You are a cowardly dog."

The entire struggle happened so quickly, yet unfolded so slowly, like a split-second that lasted a year. I couldn't breathe and my eyes grew dim and dark. I saw vulture wings closing around me, enveloping me.

I alternated between tearing at the strap with my fingers and swinging wildly at Omo with my fists. Finally, in one last act of desperation, with my pistol still wedged inside my pocket, I tried to aim the gun upward toward my foe, and pulled the trigger.

Six hollow point bullets burst out of my pants pocket in rapid succession. The first two exploded into Omo's intestines, and the third bullet shattered his kneecap as he recoiled and slung me hard away from himself. The fourth projectile dinged off the silver tea kettle on the stove – somehow I remember it distinctly – and the fifth and sixth bullets tore into my own thigh as I smashed face first into the stone fireplace.

And then there was silence as still as a clock at the end of time.

I saw Ted and myself as teenagers riding dirt bikes, skipping stones on the New River, and winding down mountain roads in his sputtering '57 Dodge. I saw Emily dancing in the rain. I saw my mother hanging curtains. I saw my father in a smoky haze, silently nursing a beer and cigarette, mourning things I would never know. I felt the stiff wind in Salinas, heard echoes in Moab, and tasted the salty sea in Coronado. I saw Tessa laughing with mustard on her chin.

April 27, 1979

I had that dream again, the one where I was walking slowly through a field of grain, and the stalks were blowing gently in a mild breeze. I brushed my fingertips along their tops and felt as though I knew them personally, each and every golden cluster. The sky was the most brilliant white that could ever be imagined, and it seemed *a living thing*, whispering to me, comforting me. There were beautiful, gently rolling hills, all of them filled with golden grain that stretched off into eternity.

But there was one thing different about the dream this time. On a not-so-distant knoll, my mother stood, waving at me timidly. She was smiling; the hard lines gone from her face. I waved and smiled back, and she disappeared.

I woke and blinked up at a white ceiling. Sunlight streamed through a large window to my right and I tried to turn toward it, but my neck was stiff and sore. The movement set my head to pounding in both temples like two hammers on one nail.

Someone whispered, "Brunky? Can you hear me?" It sounded like Tessa, but I couldn't quite get my eyes to focus.

Yes, I can hear you, I attempted to say, but my mouth would not obey my brain.

Tessa leaned in close, put a hand softly on my cheek, and said, "I'm right here, Brunky. Can you hear me?"

"Yes, I hear you," I said at last, my voice hoarse and weak.

Tessa's eyes were wet and her lips were trembling.

"Where am I?" I asked. "What happened?"

Tessa answered in short statements, pausing between each one to regroup. "You're in the hospital. You had a concussion. You've been unconscious. We didn't know if…"

I mustered a smile and put my hand on hers clumsily. "And you've been at my bedside the whole time?"

"Of course," Tessa answered, hugging me tightly, crying softly on my chest. "You did the same for me."

"Ah, so you did it out of obligation?" I said, joking gently with her, hoping to stop her tears.

Tessa rose up abruptly, put her hands on her hips, and gave me that adorable smirk of hers. Then she unleashed her rant. "You're such an idiot. None of this would have happened if you had just listened to me to begin with. You nearly died and we didn't even know where you were. We had people scouring the entire area. Do you have any idea how worried I was? Do you? And Two Arrows, too. You put us through hell. I don't know whether to smack you or kiss you."

I thought about that for a moment and studied her eyes. Finally, I said, "Well, if I must choose between those two options, I'd rather you kiss me."

And so she did.

April 30, 1979

The next time I woke up I was starving, and Tessa was asleep in a chair beside my hospital bed.

"Hey, you awake?" I whispered hoarsely.

Startled, she sat up quickly. "What? Yes, Brunky, I'm here. Are you okay?"

I smiled. "What's a guy got to do to get something to eat around here?"

Tessa jumped up excitedly. "This is great – you're awake and you've got your appetite! I'll get somebody in here right away."

"Hey, it's not that urgent," I said, trying to calm her down. But it was no use.

Tessa pushed the call button over and over for the nurses' station; then leaned out the door and shouted down the hallway, "Hey, we need some food in here quick."

In a minute, a plump, frizzy-haired nurse – her name was Hilda, according to her identification tag – with a scrunched up face appeared. "Okay, what's the problem? What's all the shouting about?"

"Brunky's awake," Tessa said. "He finally woke up again and he's hungry. I think he should eat something right away to get his strength up."

Hilda looked skeptically over the top of her glasses and cleared her throat a bit. Moving about deliberately and humming to herself, she fiddled with the monitors and IV bag by the bed, and manually checked my pulse and temperature.

Impatient, Tessa said, "Well, aren't you going to give him something? I mean, look how pale he is."

Hilda gave Tessa a look of reprimand. "Young lady, I will speak with the doctor on duty and see if she will allow Mr. Brunk to eat; and if so, what type of food he'll be permitted to have."

"How about if I get some chips and candy bars from the vending machine?" Tessa offered.

Hilda gave her another look of admonishment, one even more dreadful than the first. "You will do no such thing. Just be patient; I will have the doctor come in right away." And with that, she left the room.

When the nurse was gone, Tessa cast a disdainful look in the direction the woman had taken, and mocked her sardonically with a nasally, high-pitched voice, "You will do no such thing."

"It's okay, Tessa," I said with a laugh. "I can wait a few more minutes. They'll probably only give me chicken broth and Jell-O, but even that sounds really good right about now."

Shortly, a small team of medical personnel entered the room. "Well, hello, Mr. Brunk," a cheery, dark-haired woman said. "I'm Doctor Livingston. It's great to see you awake again. You're looking much better. The nurse tells me you're hungry. That's a good sign. A very good sign, indeed."

The doctor spoke in rapid-fire sentences. I couldn't have gotten a word in even if I'd wanted to. She and her assistants moved about me, checking vitals, touching and probing me, making notes.

"Ah, yes, things are looking just fine, indeed. Much better," the good doctor said. "Now, tell me, Mr. Brunk, who is the President of the United States?"

I shook my head uncertainly. "Uh, what does that have to do with anything?"

252

Dr. Livingston smiled at me. "Just routine questions. Can you tell me who our President is?"

I rolled my eyes and said, "Roosevelt."

Everyone in the room stopped what they were doing and looked at me.

"Ah, I guess you need me to specify which one. I'm going to say...Teddy."

"Stop it, Brunky," Tessa whispered. Then, turning to the doctor, she said, "He's being a smartass."

Dr. Livingston smiled. "Well, I'm going to take that as a good sign."

"Yeah, well, he's a lot easier to get along with when he's asleep," Tessa smirked.

"How about we order you something to eat?" Dr. Livingston said. "Are you still hungry?"

"I could eat a pizza, a steak, a chocolate milkshake, some broccoli casserole, and a bologna sandwich," I answered.

The doctor said, "I was thinking more along the lines of chicken broth and green gelatin."

"That was going to be my next choice."

"Alright, we'll get that up to you shortly," Dr. Livingston said. "And I'll be back around to check on you again in just a little while."

After the doctor and her entourage left, Tessa sat down on the bed beside me. "I'm so glad you're okay. You went back to sleep again for more than a day, and I was starting to worry again."

"Everything's going to be alright, Tess," I said. "I feel so much better now; I really do."

Tessa's hand was trembling as she caressed my forehead. "We'll get you healed up and out of here soon. Then we can get on with our lives, go somewhere new and put all of this behind us."

"Yes, no more of the darkness, anger, or revenge," I said. "Now that Omo is dead we can move on."

Tessa gave me the strangest look I'd ever seen on her face.

"What's wrong?" I asked.

"Omo's *dead*?"

"Yes, of course he is. I shot him."

"What are you talking about?" Tessa asked, looking ever more puzzled. "What makes you think you shot him?"

I thought about it for a moment. My mind was still a little foggy and disoriented, but I was certain I was remembering correctly.

I recounted the story to her bit by bit as it came back to me: "I struggled with him...he had me around the neck...yes, with my binoculars strap. And I remember trying to get my gun out of my pocket...but I couldn't..." My voice trailed off as I stared straight ahead at nothing, thinking hard.

"Are you sure?" Tessa asked carefully. "I mean, could it be that maybe...just maybe you dreamed all this while you were unconscious?"

"I did *not* dream it," I said, annoyed that she would even suggest it. "It truly happened. Omo was crushing my windpipe...I was about to die."

"Yeah, the doctors did mention your neck," Tessa interjected. "But you had so many different injuries that we were more worried about, especially the concussion and all the blood you'd lost."

I continued, "At the very last second, I pulled the trigger while the gun was still in my pocket. I saw Omo get hit and go down. I don't really know how many times I fired, but it must have been a lot. Why don't you believe me? I mean, you saw his body there, right? Who did you think shot him?"

Nervously, Tessa bit her lower lip. "Well, Brunky, the truth is…"

"What?" I said, cutting her off. "Are you telling me his body *wasn't* there? That's impossible. I shot him several times right in the gut at point blank range. And who knows where else I got him."

Tessa shook her head slowly.

"And even if that didn't kill him, there was the poison from the snake bite!" I argued.

Tessa raised her eyebrows and studied me dubiously. "*Snake bite?*"

"You think I'm crazy, don't you? Or that I must have been hallucinating."

"Brunky, I just—"

"Wait a minute," I said, my voice jumping up a notch. "What about Opal? I forgot all about her until just now. She can tell you what happened."

"Who is Opal?"

"Opal was Omo's companion or something…I'm not exactly sure. But when I got there, he had her tied down to a table, and was abusing and torturing her. I probably saved her life because I really think he would have killed her."

"Brunky, please listen to me," Tessa said softly. "There was no sign of anybody else in or around that cabin when we found you. And it looked like you'd shot yourself in the leg. Twice."

I was completely stunned by what I was hearing. "Tessa, you have to believe me; I swear I'm telling you the truth. And why in the world would I shoot myself in the leg?"

"I don't know."

Suddenly very tired, I lay my head back on the pillow and sighed deeply. "I just don't understand any of this…"

Tessa put her arms around me ever so tenderly and whispered, "It's okay, Brunky. We'll figure it all out, I promise."

I nodded weakly.

"Just rest until your food gets here. You'll feel better after you've had a little something to eat."

"You're probably right," I said. "Thank you for being here with me."

Tessa smiled. "Where else would I be? I love you."

"I love you, too."

I said the words without hesitation, surprised by how easily they flowed, and how natural they sounded to my own ears. Embracing Tessa, I felt her heart beating with mine, and the joy was unlike anything I'd ever known.

I closed my eyes, prepared for peace and bliss; but Omo was there, lurking in the darkness, waiting for me.

Brunky and Ted (1977)

www.ingramcontent.com/pod-product-compliance
Lightning Source LLC
Chambersburg PA
CBHW060147180626
46813CB00007B/2675